Wishy Washy's
Wish

May 25, 2020

for Nikko,

as we all shelter in place,
we continue to train
ourselves for our
future contributions!

Wishing All Well!

Rivkah Sweedler

Wishy Washy's Wish

Written and Illustrated by

Walter H. Barkas II
& Rivkah Sweedler

To order additional copies of this book, contact:
Xlibris Corporation
1-888-7-XLIBRIS
www.Xlibris.com
Orders@Xlibris.com
11044

Contents

WISHY WASHY'S WISH IS FOR
THE CHILDREN OF THE WORLD.
IT IS A WISH FOR AWARENESS
OF THE WIDE RANGE OF HUMAN SKILLS
AND POSSIBILITIES, AS WELL AS,
THE FREEDOM AND THE RESPONSIBILITY
INCLUDED WITH THAT AWARENESS.

Introduction

The story, set in the deep forests of the Pacific Northwest, is both environmentally educational and entertaining. Sue and Sam are 6 inch tall hand carved wood dolls who are magically brought to life by Wishy Washy Witch, the master craftswoman of the story. The mystery and suspense of Sue and Sam's survival in the woods is enhanced by detailed descriptions of basic cabin living skills and simple stick construction techniques which children can imitate. Through illustrations, photos, words and pictographs, the story presents skill-building lessons in the basic use of sticks and knot-tying: the children learn to construct ladders and lean-to's, tripods and tepees. In the process, they become familiar with Northwest plants and animals during Sue and Sam's adventures.

Acknowledgments

Wishy Washy's Wish was created and illustrated collaboratively. The actual writing of the final story was primarily Walter's work. This story and the larger scope of the project it involves have grown out of a shared living adventure and collaboration between Walter H. Barkas II and myself. This began in 1978 and seems to be continuing even after Walter's death in 1995.

We are both college graduates, products of the "Dominant Culture." When it came to living the life of simple pleasures of one's own creation, we were still "babes in the woods."

The basic human skills presented in this story and involved in creating and presenting the art and the book, were learned by us through trial and error experimentation, researching books in the library, and the generous teaching of those in our community with these various skills. Walter had been exposed to many skills while in the Peace Corp in Nigeria and while living among the Mayans in the Yucatan.

Cora Chase (1898-1983) and Corwin Chase (1897-1988) were significant mentors in the life style and skills.

An Artist Trust Gap Grant in 1988 and Washington State Arts Commission Artists-in-Residence opportunity in our local elementary school, enabled us to evolve the skills necessary to document and present our stories, art and life skills. A grant from Artist Fellowship, Inc. assisted after Walter's death.

Many have contributed to this project. Any accomplishments are truly the result of a generous and cooperative community including the Key Center Library,Morningstar Waldorf School, Evergreen and Vaughn Elementary Schools. Edie Morgan, Megan Keith, Linda Barkas, Debe Davis, Toni Freeman,Charley Launer, Steve and Kristi Nebel, Pat Semon, Aiko Watson, Harold Forche, Ed Jernberg and Mel Curtis provided early wordsmithing, documentation and presentation of our evolving work. Rick Kendig, Rosalie Thomas Cox, Marcia Levine, Gene Battell, Bea Pruski, the Lewellen, Walker, Shaufler, Gainor-Kos families and the Almanac Fund provided essential support.

Our "Well Wishers" are too numerous to mention here, but their support and belief have kept this project going through the roughest of times.

Much gratitude for assistance in the preparation and editing of the manuscript over the years , goes to Jerry and Victoria Sweedler, "Harmony Associates," "Fidelio," Ruth Rickert, Sylvia Hart, Clark Allard, and Peter and Babs McCorison.

"Disanimation,"© the more extensive illustrative process which is part of the larger "Wishy Washy Project", owes much of its evolution to the generous and creative work of Charlee Glock-Jackson and Richard Kraemer.

The beautifully haunting music by Dianne Everson plays through my head, often at times when I need to be reminded of the positive attitude of Wishy Washy.

Loving care and transportation of the life-size sculptural animals has been provided by Donna Smith-Daily and Arleen Lonning. The stovepipe was created by Mike Walker.

Teachers Bobbi Frankel, Bob Kepler, Daphne Walker, Maryjane Robbins and Nina Randolph have participated with their students over the years of evolving and refining the presentation.

Special thanks to the many teachers and children who have participated. With their enthusiasm and written and verbal feedback they have encouraged us to continue.

Marilyn Nugent and Ruth Brockmann created for our sculptural animals their eyes of fused glass. Ruth, through her own eyes, gave to us the larger understanding of our vision.

Mia McEldowney of the former MIA Gallery in Seattle, also recognized our vision as presented in our sculptures. It was she who opened many doors. She provided the opportunity to present our story and characters at the 1995 Northwest Folklife Festival just weeks before Walter died.

Walter credited his story telling to his mother, Borghild Refling Barkas, and in retrospect thought "Sue" and "Sam" were influenced by "Keri" and "Dub" of his mother's stories.

I took guidance in the process of creating a children's story from the unfinished but wonderful "In the Realm of the Talking Forest" by my cousin, Mark Pianin (1951-1983).

I was inspired by my desire to create something for my own daughters, Hilary, Marci and Jesica Sweedler Chentow, who were good sports as they lived through and put up with the learning stages as we gained the skills which eventually evolved into this book.

I am very grateful to have shared this adventure with Walter. He was an incredible guide down the forest path of living life simply, creatively, with joy and pleasure. The animals, Dido, Ahmed, Patina, Bisquit, Marley, Cider, Honey, Ikat and Sugarplum deserve much credit for their daily participation and humor.

The final acknowledgment goes to App Applegate, who came along with his sailboat on the side of the mountain to show that perhaps if there are not "Happily Ever Afters," at least the adventure of the fairy tale continues on with positive possibilities.

Rivkah Sweedler

PROLOGUE—
the Lake

A formation of mallards approaches the lake from the north. They circle clockwise and in a tightening spiral come in for a splash landing. Other birds are active on the lake this summer too. A blue heron croaks and flaps its wings at the raucous ducks. A family of mergansers have hatched and grown up here. Kingfishers dive on their prey from overhanging limbs, and at the higher level, hawks search for theirs. Swallows, woodpeckers and a dozen small birds, even hummingbirds look for food throughout the environments of water and shore. Canada geese drop in now and then, and in summer, bandtail pigeons call from the surrounding woods.

Trout leap from the surface of the lake to snap at insects on summer evenings just as swallows skim low over the water pursuing the same food. Newts, brown with orange bellies, swim to the surface with leisurely tail wags, and dive again. Frogs haunt the margins of the lake.

Numerous streams flow into Lake Washing. None large. One stream flows out of Lake Washing. The waters of the lake are enjoyed by beavers, otters, muskrats and raccoons. The shoreline is a thicket of willow and blackberry backed by a forest of mostly fir trees. Elsewhere grass grows to the water's edge, and even in the water, to the delight of the muskrats.

Deer come out of the woods to browse in these grassy areas. Mice and rabbits eat here too, which attracts foxes and coyotes, bobcats, hawks and owls.

Here and there around the lake the shoreline is hidden by dense growths of cattails.

People also live near this lake, in fact, there is a town, Washingtown. It was founded in 1859 by Willard Washing who was captivated by the country around the lake. He traded a wagonload of bottle medicine to the Indians for a large tract of land surrounding the lake.

The mountains beyond the lake harbored a small goldrush in the 1860's. Willard Washing, seeing an opportunity, opened a laundry using available Chinese laborers left over from a railroad job. The laundry served the miners in the diggings for two years at which time the gold rush gave out. Soon after, Willard Washing sold out and moved to the East with a tidy sum.

When Willard Washing retired to the East, he left behind at the lake his grown son, William. When he sold out, he sold the laundry, located on a creek near its outlet to the lake, and some surrounding acreage. Much of the remaining land around the lake was passed on by Willard to his son, at least according to some, though the whole legality of this ownership and transfer are supported by the meagerest of frontier documents. Appropriately, perhaps, because the value of such remote real estate, with no known valuable minerals and far from markets, was not great.

William Washing married a woman his own age who was left behind by the collapsing gold rush. Her name was Rosemary, and she brought as her dowry to William, a recipe for making soap.

By this time William worked a small farm, operated the only trading post in the region, and served as Justice of the Peace, Postmaster and Indian Agent.

The area of the former laundry and adjacent three hun-

dred acres had been bought site unseen by eastern specula-
tors who quickly resold it through newspaper advertisements.
People started to arrive and the beginnings of a town was
hewn from the forest and built of its logs. There was a livery
stable and blacksmith shop, a doctor's office, meeting hall,
general store and printer's. There was a community school
and adult education. The people who bought this land were
all members of an Utopian community. The town's business
was for the most part supported by travelers passing through
on the way to somewhere else.

After William and Rosemary were married, Rosemary
began making soap from her recipe. As time went by, she
improved it with the addition of mint and other herbs from
the lakeshore.

This soap became so popular both locally and with travelers that William and Rosemary started a soap factory em-
ploying a half dozen locals. The labels on the big greenish
bars said "Rosemary's Washing Soap". Business was good from
the start.

Let it be noted at this time that the territory of
Washingtown did not border directly on the lake. In those
days, owing to fear of disease, malaria, bad vapors, people did
not seek a site near water. Therefore the lakeshore land remained property of the Washings.

As years went by life around Lake Washing changed im-
perceptibly. The Indians won a limited stretch of lakeshore
as part of their reservation, from the Washing estate.

New businesses and new people moved into
Washingtown. There was logging, and a furniture factory.
The ideals of the Utopian community were forgotten by the
children, those that didn't move away when they grew up. Of
course there was a school run by the State, not the community. There was a cemetery.

But the Washing family did not grow. Each generation
barely succeeded in passing on the name to the next.

By the time of this writing, four generations since Willard Washing was here, the family consists of one unmarried daughter living on family land outside of Washingtown and near the lake.

She sold all her shares of soap factory stock to a workers' cooperative, with the proceeds in trust to pay her property taxes.

The result is, now there is an eccentric hermit woman living in the woods at the fringe of society and with virtual ownership (shared with the Indians) and responsibility for the splendid lake which bears her family name. She has spent her entire life on the shore of this lake and has grown very close to its animals, plants and natural secrets. She receives many books through the mail, or carried by travelers. Her name is Wishy Washing, but everyone fondly calls her Wishy Washy because of her open-mindedness and willingness to change her mind as new facts and evidences present themselves. It is said she studies magic things, and children call her the Wishy Washy Witch . . .

I

ABOUT THE WISHY WASHY WITCH

She was called the Wishy Washy Witch because she worked with wishing and with washing and because she seemed to have the power to do things that others could not do. It was agreed by all that she was definitely in the category of "Good Witches"! As for the "Wishy Washy", this too was with admiration for her willingness to change and admit when something proves to be wrong.

She lived apart from other people, off in the woods with her animals on a little road named Witch Way and so carved on a rustic sign.

As for the washing, she had an ancient washing machine

that made wonderful noises as it danced back and forth in agitation, such sounds as made the Witch dance for joy herself sometimes. She did a lot of other things that other people do as well.

She cared for her animals. They were a donkey, two goats, two dogs and two cats. She gathered firewood and other things she needed from the woods. She tended her herb garden.

Now as for the wishing, in this was her special work that no one else did.

In front of the Wishy Washy Witch's house there was a wishing well. Most people called it "Witching Well," and believed that if you dropped small offerings of money or other valuables into the well and made a wish, well, that wish might be granted.

The Wishy Washy Witch felt a tremendous responsibility for this well and its powers. From it she drew not only her water, but a small but steady income of coins and other interesting things. She called this her "well-fare," but she worried that people would wish for things that might do more harm than good. What about someone who wished for rain to settle the dust and temper the summer heat just when farmers were trying to get their hay dry in the sun before storing it in the barns? What would the animals eat in winter if it spoiled?

So, the Wishy Washy Witch had built a fence around the well, with a gate and a bell, and two benches facing each other under a split shake roof.

When someone would ring the well bell, the Witch would come out and sit with the person on the benches, drink the water and talk about wishes and what their consequences might be. If after talking over the wish with the Witch the person still wanted to wish for it, why the Witch opened the gate to the well and wished them well!

She called this "washing wishes" and not only was she able to feel she'd dealt responsibly with the powers of the

well, but she was able to keep up with the happenings in
other people's lives through hearing about their wishes.

The well did not answer all wishes, or at least not in ways
that the people realized at the time. Sometimes wishes weren't
granted until years later.

One year Wishy Washy heard a wish that wasn't wished
because of the well at all, but because of the washing machine. Santa Claus stopped by to pick up some laundry that
Wishy Washy had done for him.

Santa said "All these dolls are wearing me out! I have to
take so many millions of dolls, different kinds of dolls, to the
children all over the world. Just to get them properly dressed
and organized by country in my toy bag is work for two people,
maybe two small people, anyway, I sure wish I had some doll
helpers."

With that, Santa gave candy canes to Wishy Washy and to
each of her animals, and taking his laundry sack on his back
like a bag of toys, he boarded his sleigh and was gone like a
vanishing mist.

II

HOW SUE AND SAM WERE MADE

Wishy Washy Witch thought about Santa's wish for a long time, then one day, sitting by the well, she decided she might have the answer. Santa's work was so good, bringing gifts to people all over the world. Surely a gift for Santa, to help him in his work, would have special power that pure goodness would bring.

Wishy Washy was a skillful wood carver. She planned to carve a pair of wooden dolls to be Santa's helpers in the doll department. But in order to be of any help, they would have to be very special dolls. They would have to come alive. From her witch knowledge, she believed that three ingredients might make the magic of coming alive happen. The first was the power of goodness. The second was the wood from which the dolls were carved. Wishy Washy had a large limb broken from the tree of knowledge during a windstorm. She had saved this limb with the carving wood in her barn for a long time for just such a special purpose. The knowledge in the wood would give intelligence and wisdom to her dolls and the ability to learn. The third ingredient was a magic chant that Wishy Washy had written down in her notebook when she was learning witch things long before.

She cut some pieces of the tree of knowledge wood that were the right size to make two small dolls, and put them into a leather pouch.

Later, at home, after her animals were tended, Wishy Washy studied the pieces of wood and thought about how to make the dolls. With her hatchet, she split some of the wood into the right thickness to become arms and legs. Two pieces would make the head and body of each doll. On each of these she carved a deep notch all the way around to mark what would be the neck of each doll, and give her a place to start from next time. Then she drilled holes through the wooden pieces so that the arms and legs could be attached to the bodies. As she did this, she recited the chant to make the dolls come alive:

> "Fallen branch from a special tree,
> carved with love into what you'll be.
> Song of springtime, song of fall.
> Growth rings circle through them all.
> Painted eyes so you can see.
> Gently shaped, your limbs move free.
> Summer sun and winter snow.
> Through your learning you will grow."

That finished, she put the doll wood into the pouch and went about a few chores she had to do before bedtime, such as splitting kindling for the morning fire.

The next day, as on several that followed, she took the doll pouch with her to the woods when she brought her goats and donkey out to browse on berry vines, willow shoots, ferns and the like.

She went deep into the woods where it was quiet save for bird calls. There, instead of gathering mushrooms or berries or wild herbs as she might have, she carved on the dollies. She had her pocket knife, sharpening stone and a bit of sandpaper. Here she worked for an hour or so while the animals browsed, always ending with the chant.

> "Fallen branch from a special tree,
> carved with love into what you'll be.
> Song of springtime, song of fall.
> Growth rings circle through them all.
> Painted eyes so you can see.
> Gently shaped, your limbs move free.
> Summer sun and winter snow.
> Through your learning you will grow."

Then she and her dogs, Marley and Bisquit, would bring the animals home again.

One day, when she was close to finishing the dolls, she put in extra work sitting by her barn, and got the last of the carving done and smoothed them with a white stone. The dolls were ready for the final touches on the following day.

Next morning, when it was time to take the animals out, as usual she unlocked the well gate and put up a 'welcome' sign, as she allowed people who really wanted to make a wish to do so without her. If they wanted to talk, they waited for her return.

In an extra bag, she brought glue, scissors, paint and a

brush to finish the dolls. Once again donkey, goats, witch
and dog walked off along a forest path until they came to an
opening under large cedar trees.

The donkey was shedding his winter coat. Wishy Washy
had only to comb her fingers through his fur to come up with
half a handful of loose hair. She glued some of this on the
dolls' heads. Next she attached the arms and legs so that
they could move. Finally, she painted the eyes. Then, placing the dolls carefully side by side in the leather pouch, she
hung it on a branch to let the paint dry. She recited the
chant:

> "Fallen branch from a special tree,
> carved with love into what you'll be.
> Song of springtime, song of fall.
> Growth rings circle through them all.
> Painted eyes so you can see.
> Gently shaped, your limbs move free.
> Summer sun and winter snow.
> Through your learning you will grow."

She was just sitting back to admire the dolls' faces when
she realized how uncomfortable she was. Ants! Hundreds of
them!

Wishy Washy had been sitting on a log that was nearly
hollow from the work of many ants who had eaten the wood
inside. They had come out to see who Wishy Washy was, and
climbed all over her and into her clothes while she had been
busy at work. They tickled and she itched as they bit her.
Wishy Washy shrieked and danced and ran off homeward to
change her clothes, letting the animals keep up as best they
could.

III

How Sue and Sam Were Lost

Arriving home out of breath, the Wishy Washy Witch was glad to find no one waiting to wash wishes. She hurried to change her clothes and brush off the ants, and then she hung her old clothes outside so that the remaining ants could leave them.

Only after this was done did she remember Sue and Sam, the names she had thought of for the dolls while she was finishing them. Wishy Washy remembered leaving them hanging in their pouch in the distant cedar grove.

The donkey and both goats were waiting outside her door for the treat she usually gave them when they came home from their walk. On that day she had some cookies, made the night before with oatmeal and molasses. The animals eagerly followed Wishy Washy to their barn where she led them with the cookies and shut them in. She had to run back to the cedar grove for the dolls before something happened to them, and if the animals were free to follow, it would only slow her down. The Witch called for Marley and Bisquit. When they did not appear immediately, she set off for the woods alone at a fast walk.

When Marley saw the Witch jump up from her seat in the cedar grove and run off beating at the ants, he was alarmed. But Marley was also an observant and loyal dog. He knew that the pouch left hanging on a branch was something of value. He jumped up to seize the strap in his teeth and carry it along after the Witch, donkey and goats.

The pouch, with its dolls inside, kept getting caught on snagging branches and disallowed doggish short cuts through the underbrush. Marley was soon left far behind the other animals but refused to drop his burden.

Then, coming around a turn in the path, Marley came face to face with a skunk. Marley knew about skunks. He knew that his wisest move would be retreat. Before he was able to make any move, however, the skunk turned its back and released a cloud of stinking, choking vapor right at the unfortunate dog. Temporarily blinded, Marley dived into the underbrush beside the path and dragged himself and the pouch through it for a long ways before he recovered his senses. Using every bit of his doggish sense of direction, Marley found his way back to the path that led homeward, just in time to meet Wishy Washy Witch, on her way back to find Sue and Sam.

"Good dog, Marley, you've got my pouch!" said the Witch. "But where are Sue and Sam, and what's all this skunk smell about?" For now the pouch was empty and stinking of skunk. Sue and Sam were nowhere to be seen.

Wishy Washy Witch and Marley followed the path back to the cedar grove and the ant log. On the way they passed the spot where Marley had met the skunk. There was still no sign of Sue and Sam. Wishy Washy Witch moaned, "Oh, now I've no gift for Santa, and Sue and Sam are lost in the woods!"

Marley's nose and eyes were still so inflamed from the skunking that she knew he couldn't help her find them. Also, Wishy Washy knew that those dolls, endowed with the three ingredients, the power of goodness, the wood from the tree of knowledge, and the magic chant, were all ready to come alive. Wishy Washy knew that once off the path, Marley could've lost them anywhere. She had to search for them.

Wishy Washy climbed over logs and pushed through brush. She crawled through thickets of berry stalks and nettles with no success. She called the names, "Sue" and "Sam". Time passed and her search grew more weary.

Then she brushed a tree branch that carried a nest of hornets, called yellow jackets because of their attire.

The yellow jackets defended their nest fiercely. They dived on Wishy Washy , circling her head for an opening in her flailing arms. They flew up her skirt, they got in her hair. They stung terribly, this was worse than the ants!

Wishy Washy yelled and fled through the woods, chased by the insects. By the time she regained the path, the yellow jackets had left her, but Wishy Washy had at least a half dozen burning stings on various parts of her body. It was all she could manage to continue on home and give up on Sue and Sam for the day. Marley sadly followed.

IV

How Sue and Sam
Come Alive

Sue and Sam lay still not far
from each other on the forest floor. A deep carpet of fallen,
rotting leaves layered the ground around the bases of bushes
and trunks of trees. Eventually something wonderful began
to happen.

The dolls gradually started to awaken. Since they'd never
been alive, except as wood from the branch of the tree of
knowledge, they had no memory, and no understanding of
what was happening to them.

Sam blinked his eyes, and saw the forest scene around

him. Sue also saw, but moved her legs and arms as well. As time passed, the two dolls gathered their strength and wits like butterflies emerging from cocoons to stretch their wings and fly away.

Although Sue and Sam knew nothing of their origins, they had within them some image of the Wishy Washy Witch. They also recognized each other and knew that they belonged together. They stood and stretched, and walked. They swung their arms, wiggled their fingers and nodded their heads.

"I'm Sue," said Sue. "And I am Sam," said Sam.

With that, they found that they could talk, and quickly found many things to talk about. Mostly it was questions about who they were, where they were and why.

The two dolls also found that they were hungry, but didn't know what to do about it, even though a large, olive drab slug lay nibbling a mushroom nearby and watching Sue and Sam through his stalk-eyes.

Darkness came to the deep shadows under the bushes. The dolls lay down where they were and slept. An owl hooted and the moon rose.

Gradually it grew lighter. Bird calls sounded from tree tops around the two dolls. Sue stirred from where she lay and sat up. She looked toward Sam, and in the dim dawn's light she saw a mysterious shape right on top of Sam. She called his name in alarm, and Sam too stirred, or tried to.

The slug which had watched them earlier had been curious and had come to examine Sam in the night. By now it had decided that he was an inedible, uninteresting piece of wood, and was gliding slowly over his body in search of a better breakfast. Every time Sam squirmed, the slug contracted in alarm and stopped moving.

Only after Sam lay still in exhaustion and disgust did the wandering gastropod proceed in its leisurely crossing of Sam's body, and finally glide off on its own business. A silver trail marked the meandering of the slug from the mushroom, across Sam and on to where the slug was climbing an old tree stump.

"How awful," said Sam, "I've got this revolting slime on me!"

Sue agreed that it was disgusting stuff. They tried to wipe it off with leaves, but that didn't work. The leaves got stuck in it.

The two dolls, who'd just come to life, were totally lost, and had no idea what to do. A faint animal path led away under the bushes.

Sue said, "Maybe this way goes somewhere better than where we are."

So Sue and Sam took their first walking steps along this path, over tree roots and under vines. The path led them to a place where huge cedar trees grew and the underbrush disappeared.

Through the center of the cedar grove, a tiny stream of water wandered among ancient mossy roots and logs, sometimes disappearing underground, to reappear a few yards further along. Large leafed devil's clubs and skunk cabbage grew along this watercourse as well as a profusion of ferns.

Sue and Sam met water for the first time. At a sandy bottomed pool they learned to drink and swim, and handsful of sand with water and moss scrubbed the slug slime from Sam's body.

Now Sue and Sam were in some ways like real living people, in other ways they were not. For instance cold hardly bothered them, and they did not feel pain. But they did feel hunger, which fact Sue and Sam were just starting to discover. They watched a bird pick and eat berries and a squirrel open fir cones and eat the tiny seeds inside. Sue and Sam each found berries which had been knocked down by the birds and ate them.

Once fed, Sue and Sam decided that they needed a place to rest where they wouldn't get run over by slugs again.

Sue noticed an opening in a tree trunk that seemed like the perfect place, but it was too high for the dolls to reach. Sue stood on Sam's shoulders, and still could not reach the opening. What to do?

V

THE WISHY WASHY WITCH
AND HER MAGIC SCREEN

All this time the Wishy Washy
Witch had been worrying and working to find Sue and Sam.
Her plan made use of a tool—her magic screen, and an ally,
Sugarplum.

Wishy Washy Witch's magic screen had been given to
her by her father. It was accompanied by a book on its use and
care. With it also came a "scene stone." When one pointed
the stone at the magic screen and said certain magic words
from the book, scenes of far away, or long ago, or both or of
the future would appear. By thinking very hard of what one
wanted to see, why, the scene on the screen would become

that thing or something close to it. However, the magic screen used this way did not have its full powers. Too much concentrated thinking was needed; if the person using it let his or her mind wander ever so slightly, the picture ricocheted wildly in time and space on the screen. There was no good way to aim it.

But, as the book said, if a person could find his or her own special "scene stone," and keep it near them, and if the person had an ally to be the "eyes and ears" of the screen, the full power of the magic screen was there for them.

A personal "scene stone" could not be bought. A person had to find their own, in nature. Wishy Washy'd recently found hers on a rocky beach. It was as large as her hand, and had a hollow in it that exactly fitted her thumb. The stone was a dark, reddish color, with white lines across it and tiny shining specks that might be gold. It was a very powerful stone, and with it the witch could think of a scene and hold the view of it on her screen for as long as she needed to.

Her ally was Sugarplum. Sugarplum was a Stellar's jay that Wishy Washy had saved as a fallen fledgling, and raised in her home like her own child. Sugarplum had grown up, and had flown away one day to lead a jay's life. However, Wishy Washy was the mother that Sugarplum remembered. He came back and visited her often, and frequently helped her with her witch work.

Now Wishy Washy went outside and called in jay talk, "Sugarplum, Wishy Washy needs you!"

She heard the answering screech of a jay from a hazel thicket nearby. It was not Sugarplum, but another jay who was sure to pass the message on to all the rest of the jays until it reached Sugarplum where ever in the forest he might be.

When Sugarplum arrived an hour later, he and Wishy Washy had a fond reunion and a little lunch. Then when both of them were rested and ready, she opened the velvet curtains that covered the the screen, pointed her "scene stone" at it, said the magic words and thought of Sue and Sam and the place she had last seen them.

Sugarplum sat on the witch's shoulder and thought of her until their thoughts became one. He hopped to the window and flew out and within a few minutes he landed on top of the tall cedar under which Wishy Washy had left Sue and Sam. He gazed over the forest. The scene he saw appeared on the magic screen exactly as seen through his eyes.

The dense cover of treetops, brush and ferns concealed any small objects on the ground from view. Sugarplum flew lower, down among the tree branches where reduced sunlight had kept the ground more open. Further along he came to a thicket of young fir trees growing so closely together that he could not fly between them. He flew through groves of alders, and places where willow and hazel grew among salmonberry bushes.

Entering a shadowy group of large cedar trees along a stream, Sugarplum quickly found what he sought. There stood Sam and Sue! They were at the base of one of the large cedars, which like many of its kind went on living and growing even though the center of its trunk was being devoured by termites. This fact was clear from the several holes made into it by woodpeckers. The length of the lower trunk was pierced by neat, chiseled-looking holes so that it resembled a flute.

Sue and Sam, miraculously alive, both delighted and concerned Wishy Washy as she watched them through the eyes of the jay. How could she get to them? Would they stay in one place to be found? Would they be safe?

Sugarplum dropped low to land on an ancient mossy log a few feet from Sue and Sam. Through the jay's ears the Wishy Washy Witch heard the tiny voices of Sue and Sam for the first time. She eavesdropped on their discussion about finding a safe place to sleep and watched them struggle, Sue standing on Sam's shoulders, to try to reach the lowest large woodpecker hole. This attempt failed.

Wishy Washy wanted to help them, in fact she realized that she must, as they were alone in the world and knew so little of what they needed to know to survive. She decided to write them a letter. She recited the dolls' chant:

> "Fallen branch from a special tree,
> carved with love into what you'll be.
> Song of springtime, song of fall.
> Growth rings circle through them all.
> Painted eyes so you can see.
> Gently shaped, your limbs move free.
> Summer sun and winter snow.
> Through your learning you will grow."

With her thoughts she called Sugarplum to return to her. She closed the curtains on her screen and set to work with paper and pen. She drew pictures of the things she wanted to teach.

Meanwhile Sugarplum had arrived. After offering him some refreshment of grapes and oatmeal, Wishy Washy rolled up her letter which she had drawn quite small on thin paper. She tied the rolled letter with a strip of bark and sent the bird off to deliver it.

VI

THE LETTER

Sue and Sam had become hungry and exhausted trying to reach the hole in the tree. They found a few beautiful blackberries to eat and were wondering what to do next. Then Sugarplum arrived. The black and blue bird landed first on a hazel branch and then hopped to the mossy ground in front of the two dolls. Sugarplum thrust the rolled letter at Sue until she took it. He released it to her hands, flapped his wings a bit, squawked and bristled his head crest. He flew back up to the low hazel limb and looked on.

Of course, the Wishy Washy Witch was tuned in to this

delivery and saw and heard everything through the jay's senses.

Now Sue and Sam were left with the letter. It was a big roll. On end it was half as tall as Sue or Sam. After the dolls had examined the roll thoroughly, including peering through the hollow center, they worked the cedar bark binding off one end. You can imagine their curiosity and amazement over this bird-borne bounty. They'd never seen paper before.

When they unrolled the letter they saw that there were markings inside. This didn't seem noteworthy as the two dolls had already seen leaves and tree bark marked by insects and other forces of nature. But somehow the way the Witch's pictures stood out from the pure smooth white of the paper riveted Sue and Sam's attention.

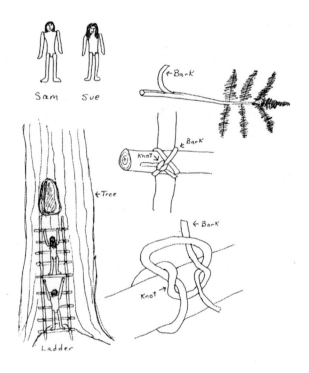

Soon Sam began to see the pictures: "Look Sue, that is us," he said pointing at the drawing of the dolls on the letter.

"And there we are climbing to the hole in the tree," said Sue, "but how?"

After some more study, Sue and Sam figured out the drawings in the letter; how to peel some bark, how to use it to lash sticks together to make a ladder. This they did, and just in time, as both thickening clouds and the lateness of the hour brought darkness nearer as they scrambled into the tree hole. Sugarplum flew off on his own business.

As the two wooden dolls were just getting comfortable in their wooden cave, Sue said, "We left our gift from the bird down there!" So, all the way down again she went, retrieved the roll of paper, and lightly ascended the ladder with the letter.

In the last of the light the two again reviewed the pictures that had taught them so much so quickly; about ladders, and strips of bark and tying knots. Perhaps their quick learning was because they were made from wood of the tree of knowledge.

That night it rained, and Sue and Sam were glad to be in their tree hole which was high above the wet ground and the slugs.

With the morning light the sound of rain changed to that of dripping trees. Before long the clouds opened and sun shone down on the forest. Through gaps in the tree tops Sue and Sam saw a rainbow, and watched it in wonder until it faded.

As the two were thinking of going down the ladder to look for berries, they heard a loud pounding noise above them. Pieces of wood fell in front of their doorway. When the racket stopped, Sue and Sam cautiously looked out and up. They saw a big black bird, with a red and white head and neck. It gripped the tree trunk with its claws and began hammering away again at another hole higher up the tree. Chips of wood flew. Sue and Sam pulled in their heads.

Sam said "Sue, this whole tree must belong to that bird.

We had better leave it before he makes us into little chips! We'll have to find another place for ourselves.

"It would certainly be good to be able to cut wood the way that bird does!" observed Sue.

Sue and Sam descended and wandered towards the stream in search of berries. They found many salal berries in one bunch. Sue suggested that if they made a thing like a small ladder, they could pile the bunches of berries on it. They could carry it with them by the two ends. They continued their walk with this load in the direction in which they had seen the rainbow and following the stream.

After some time had passed, Sugarplum appeared again, and again on a hazel branch. This time he carried no letter, but set to work pecking at the hazel nuts on some of the branches. Sue and Sam were ready to rest, so they sat and watched the jay.

Sugarplum cracked and ate a few nuts, then cracked and dropped a few to the dolls. They tried eating the nuts and found then delicious and the halves of broken shell seemed useful too.

Sugarplum dropped a nut without cracking it. The two dolls beat on it with their hands, and with sticks, without damaging it.

Finally they rolled it to the stream where there were rocks. By placing the nut on a rock and then hitting it hard with a large rock that Sue lifted over her head they cracked it and enjoyed it. Several nuts later Sam missed the nut when he tried to crack it and split a large chip off his rock, making sparks in the process.

Pleased with the knowledge of nuts and how to crack them, Sue and Sam decided to stay for a time under the hazel tree. Since there was no obvious ready made home for them, the two dolls thought of making their own house using the skills they had learned in making their ladder.

Their idea was to build a lean-to made from sticks that they tied together with bark. Then they covered it with leaves.

Through Sugarplum, the Wishy Washy Witch looked in on Sue and Sam, and was pleased with how well they were doing.

"But," she said to Sugarplum, "There are a few things that they are ready to learn now that will make their lives easier. I think it's time to send them another letter."

And so she set to work with pen, paper and magnifying glass to draw a letter small enough that Sugarplum could carry it and the dolls handle it.

She showed Sam cracking a nut with a rock in the first picture. In the next picture she showed a large piece chipping off Sam's stone when it missed the nut. Then she drew pictures showing how the sharp chip of stone could be lashed to a wooden handle to make an ax. Using this tool would be an easier way to open nuts and to do many other things.

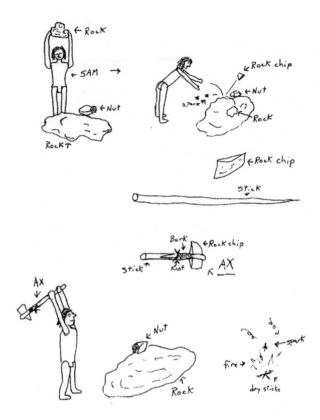

Sugarplum carried this letter to Sue and Sam's camp, where he found them harvesting hazel nuts. Once again the jay delivered his letter and flew to a nearby perch to observe the reaction, and to eat a few nuts himself. These he pecked open with his strong beak.

Sue and Sam studied the pictures in the letter. It was easy to understand and an exciting idea. Sam ran to get the chip of stone from his nut cracking place, while Sue looked for an appropriate piece of wood. She found a bit of cedar branch that was broken at one end with a long tapering tip which could be bent around the stone as in the picture. The dolls peeled a long strip of cedar bark as well. Then Sam placed the stone on the stick and bent the tip around it and held it in place while Sue wrapped it with bark into a tight lashing. She finished with the knot they had learned in making their ladder.

The ax was wonderful! A few blows would open a hazel nut, or cut a stick. The dolls quickly decided that they each needed one. At the edge of the stream Sue found a sharp chip of black stone that looked perfect for an ax. With it they made a second ax.

Both Sugarplum and the Wishy Washy Witch were delighted to see Sue and Sam so self sufficient, for both of them had other important things happening in their lives quite apart from Sue and Sam. They were ready to leave the two dolls on their own for a while and tend to other matters.

Sue and Sam were having a wonderful time exploring the small world along the stream. There were logs to climb on, beautiful plants to explore, mossy hollows to lie in. Hazel nuts and berries were their food, and the small amount of each that the dolls could eat was easy to find.

One day they watched a squirrel remove the outer leaflets from a fir cone to get at the tiny seeds inside. Sue and Sam learned to strip a fir cone for seeds using their axes in place of the sharp teeth of the squirrel.

The squirrel placed great importance on storing away cones in tree hollows, far more cones than it could eat immediately. For Sue and Sam, this was food for thought.

On another day they found a strangely flat, smooth piece of wood with markings on it. Protruding from holes in this flat surface were two ridged posts with flat tops.

In fact they were nails in a sign that said "No Trespassing" which had come from somewhere upstream and been left behind by high water in a pile of other pieces of wood on the stream bank. By wiggling and twisting the nails, Sue and Sam were able to remove them from their holes in the sign.

Both of the nails had good, sharp points, one of them was straight, the other slightly bent. The dolls were sure that the nails were valuable things to have, so they brought them back to the lean-to to keep with their other possessions; nut shells to drink from, axes and their berry carrier.

VII

SUE AND SAM AND THE POT OF GOLD

The next morning Sue and Sam awoke in their lean-to, to begin another day of exploring, play, and collecting food. The sun fell in warm patches through openings in the tree tops, and made pleasant spots to just sit and be.

During one such interlude, while they had been playing with spider webs, Sue said, "Look over there, there is something like a piece of the rainbow!"

Indeed, on a sandbank by the side of the stream, in another patch of sunshine, something was making colors. The dolls got up from their comfortable mossy seats and started for the strange object.

The distance was greater and the going more difficult than it seemed at first. At one point they were deep in a salmonberry thicket, and Sam had to climb a tree to see which was the right direction to get to the sand bank.

Eventually they reached it. Up close the object did not show the rainbow colors that first caught Sue's attention, but the thing was very interesting just the same. It was round and smooth and slippery like a stream-washed stone, but Sue and Sam could see right through it to the other side.

It seemed to be empty inside. One end seemed to be smaller than the other, but the small end was still buried in the ground. Sue and Sam found sticks with which to dig away the compacted sand so that they could see the whole thing.

As they uncovered the small end, a beautiful cap of gold was revealed covering the end of this whole strange object, which was bigger than Sue and Sam together. Some knocking and twisting loosened the cap, and with more work it came off, revealing the sole opening in their find. The cap was beautiful, and big enough to slip on neatly over Sue or Sam's head, to be carried away. The rest of the object was far too big to move. The opening was too small for either doll to enter.

As the shadows were beginning to grow long, Sue and Sam started back towards their camp. They decided to follow the stream back, since the way they had come to reach the buried bottle, through the salmonberry thicket, though shorter, was very difficult. They happily skipped from stone to stone, occasionally wading, and leaving their footprints in sand and mud along with those of birds and animals.

At a distance they watched a raccoon climb down from a tree and wander up the stream ahead of them. In a quiet pool they watched tadpoles and water strider bugs.

The great leaves of devil's club, sword ferns and skunk

cabbage formed tents, awnings and umbrellas overhead, covering the dolls from either sun or rain. The calls and labors of both squirrels and woodpecker, now familiar to Sue and Sam, frequently sounded through the forest. Now and then a Stellar jay showed itself, sometimes a pair of them.

Sue and Sam each carried the pot of gold part of the way, worn over their heads like a hat. They also found how good it was for scooping up water and carrying it.

Sue kept feeling that her hair was getting in her eyes and mouth. She found a tiny leafy vine and bound it round her head, and then, finding a very small flower, she twisted its stem through her headband and looked at the result in the still water. She decided it looked good and went off to show it to Sam. By the time she caught up to him they were home at the lean-to.

Once rested from their walk, Sue and Sam gathered and ate more berries and nuts, and since it was nearly dark then, they rolled into their mossy beds under the lean-to roof and slept.

Daylight came with drizzling rain and a light wind that shook the water off drenched branches and leaves to fall like tossed bucketsful to the forest floor.

Sue and Sam's lean-to was built up close to the trunk of a great cedar. The drooping evergreen branches of the cedar acted almost as a thatched roof to keep the ground quite dry in a large area around the bottom of the tree. Of course, under the lean-to was perfectly dry. Out beyond their tree, however, it seemed the whole world was soaked.

As they had food close at hand, the two dolls spent the morning in the lean-to. They looked at the last letter from the jay, about breaking stones and making axes. There were things in the letter that Sue and Sam did not understand.

Sam went over to the rocky place, outside the lean-to but still protected by the tree. He threw stones down onto stones and broke off some chips that might be good for axes or other things, but this was not Sam's purpose. He wanted to see the sparks that sometimes happened when stone struck stone.

One spark landed amongst some dry cedar needles. A thin column of smoke arose from the spot. Sam got down close to see what was happening. His breath caused a tiny spark to glow brighter. Sam blew. The spark grew brighter still, then went out.

Sam called Sue and told her what had happened. Remembering the letter, Sue and Sam gathered some light, dry litter, shredded wood and bark from under a woodpecker hole and an abandoned mouse nest from a deep cavity among the cedar roots. Excited now, Sam threw stones down on others with all his strength.

Sue kept saying, "Try another one Sam, try one more," as some stones failed to spark and from others, sparks flew far from the pile of kindling. Finally one spark did land in the mouse nest, among dry grasses and thistle down.

Sam was too out of breath from his hard work to blow on it, but Sue did. The spark glowed larger, finally there was a tiny but growing flame. The fire needed more fuel. Sue and Sam fed it twigs and fir cone chips that had been left by squirrels.

They were fascinated by this thing they had made, which gave forth heat and light. Sam put his hand in it, which immediately began to smoke and scorch. He ran out into the cool rain which quickly stopped the burning.

Sue and Sam spent the rest of the day and far into the night learning about their fire. They enclosed it with stones to keep it from escaping into the dry needles on the ground. They learned to have water in the pot of gold to pour on any sparks that strayed outside their fireplace.

They stayed by the fire when night came, just to enjoy the light, and the shadows the flickering flames made on the great trunks around them. They fed it small sticks through the evening.

Finally, that night Sue and Sam learned to sing.

To begin their fireside sing, Sue said, "Listen Sam, I can be a squirrel!" and she began a high pitched trilling sound, something like a red squirrel's.

Sam chimed in with his version. Soon the two were mimicking the trills, pauses and single chirps they'd been hearing daily from their ever present woods fellows. Sam added some woodpecker calls, and tapped a rhythm on a log with his hard wooden heels.

Sue finished with a jay call and they both laughed. Soon after that they slept where they were. The rain stopped before daylight.

VIII

RUMORS OF AUTUMN

The sun rose above grey skies, but as it heated the air, the clouds disappeared. Sun struck the tall tree tops and gradually penetrated the deep forest canopy to mottle the ground with warm spots of sunlight.

Some of the leaves of the alder trees had started turning yellow, and falling, and littering the ground, the green moss and clumps of swordfern. The sunshine showed these golden among the many shades of green and brown.

The Wishy Washy Witch was up early. This was a very busy time of year because the berries, fruits, garden vegetables, wild mushrooms, even the hay were ripe now and ready for harvest all over the community. Everyone including the Wishy Washy Witch had some of this work to do. Then there was firewood to gather, roofs to patch, gutters to clean and chimneys to sweep. There were so many things to do to get ready for the cold, hungry months ahead.

This morning there was a bubbling kettle of applesauce on Wishy Washy's wood stove. She was bustling about, singing and muttering to herself as she prepared jars for the applesauce. Wishy Washy liked to get this hot stove work finished while the morning chill was still in the air and before long she was done. She had a dozen jars of applesauce with their lids sealed and cooling.

The Wishy Washy Witch went outside then, to enjoy the morning sun and to take a bowl of apple peelings and parings to her goats and donkey. Watching the animals eat and just reflecting on the nice day to come after yesterday's rain, Wishy Washy watched a jay land on a nearby fir limb.

The presence of the jay called Sue and Sam to her attention, and Wishy Washy thought that she had better check on them. She called the jay to her and sent it off with a message for Sugarplum to come to her.

While the applesauce had been cooking on top of the stove, Wishy Washy had made an apple pie and put it in the oven. By early afternoon it had baked and cooled, and Wishy Washy was just settling down to eat a piece for lunch when Sugarplum arrived. He was happy to have a small piece of pie.

Soon both Sugarplum and Wishy Washy discovered that the pie was burned on the bottom and not very sweet. Perhaps that is why the jay did not delay when Wishy Washy sent him on his way to fly over the forest and find Sue and Sam.

Sugarplum looked along the stream where he had last seen the dolls, and soon found they had not moved far.

Their tiny camp with a lean-to covered with leaves was built close up to the roots of a great cedar tree. Wishy Washy, watching through her scene screen was delighted to see a tiny wisp of smoke from a fireplace built of rocks outside the lean-to. As the jay settled on a low, dead cedar limb to watch, Sue approached the fire with a few twigs of firewood.

"So, the clever dolls figured out the message of fire!!" said Wishy Washy to herself.

Next Sam appeared carrying the pot of gold on his shoulder, filled with berries. He set them down by the fire, and picking up a sharp stick, he skewered a berry on it and held it over the glowing embers to roast. After he had rotated and roasted the berry on all sides he offered it to Sue. She grasped it in a leaf and pulled it off the skewer. It must have been good, the way she gobbled it, though it made a mess of her face.

"It must be better than my cooking," said Wishy Washy. "They really are doing all right," went on the witch to herself, "in a primitive sort of way, but I'm worried about them when winter comes if they aren't home yet by then."

For Wishy Washy was determined to be reunited with lost Sue and Sam. With much caring she chanted:

> "Fallen branch from a special tree,
> carved with love into what you'll be.
> Song of springtime, song of fall.
> Growth rings circle through them all.
> Painted eyes so you can see.
> Gently shaped, your limbs move free.
> Summer sun and winter snow.
> Through your learning you will grow."

Wishy Washy then called Sugarplum home. She sent him off about his business with a piece of pie crust.

Wishy Washy thought long on how to help Sue and Sam some more so that they could survive the cold weather to come. As she was taking out the remains of her pie to the goats she began to plan the next letter.

She decided to teach Sue and Sam to eat fish, as there

were many tiny fish in the streams. These were about the right size for Sue and Sam. Besides fishing would lead them downstream. All of the streams in the area flowed into the same lake, and Wishy Washy's home was near the shore of that lake. If they moved down to the lake shore, she'd be more likely to find them.

Wishy Washy thought that since the dolls learned to eat berries and nuts from birds and squirrels, that she would draw a kingfisher bird to teach them about fish. Wishy Washy also wanted to help them improve their pot of gold for cooking. She drew the pot with the top edges being pierced by a nail and then the pot with a handle passed through the holes, and finally, a picture of the pot hanging over a fire. When the tiny letter was finished she rolled it up and fastened it with a soft thin wire to be the pot handle.

At the moment that the Wishy Washy Witch finished her letter to Sue and Sam, she heard the Well Bell tinkle, meaning some Well-wishers had come. Marley and Bisquit barked. She thought to herself that there was no hurry to send off the letter, and that Sugarplum probably wouldn't like to have to go on another errand today anyway. So, she put the letter into a little basket that also contained her scene stone.

Out at the well were two local ladies, Mrs. Trudger, a teacher, and Ms. Weed who did many different things like painting pictures and baking cakes. They had met each other on the road, and since Mrs. Trudger had a package of dog bones she wanted to deliver to Wishy Washy anyway, both women decided to come and have a visit and make a wish at the well just for the pleasure of it.

Wishy Washy joined the two ladies to sit on the well benches and have a chat. After considerable talking about health, children, apples, dogs and other people, they all three agreed that autumn was certainly coming.

Mrs. Trudger said she wanted to wish for an easy winter, and dropping her coins in the well, did so. Ms. Weed said that she wished she could find a larger house to rent. She and her children felt too crowded in their small place. Wishy Washy reminded her that a larger house meant paying more rent almost certainly, and would mean moving away and leaving behind the things that she liked about where she was. Wishy Washy suggested that Ms. Weed and her family might all enjoy spending more time out of doors, and perhaps building a lean-to to spend time in when it rained.

Ms. Weed said, "you may be right, Wishy Washy, I guess I'll wish for an easy winter too. Look, I've got only a penny on me so I'll just chip in on Mrs. Trudger's wish, like a sale, two wishes for just one penny more!" She dropped the coin in the well and was rewarded by the sound of the distant splash.

Both ladies had to go then. Wishy Washy thanked Mrs. Trudger for the dog bones and told both of them that she'd be happy to share their easy winter.

After the two had left, Wishy Washy said aloud, "And I wish that Sue and Sam would come back to me" and dropped her own coin in the well, the same place from which Wishy Washy originally got it. She went on, "those two dollies are so clever, I'll let them decide for themselves whether they want to go work for Santa or do something else if only they come back," and she went off to start her washing machine.

IX

A TRIP TO TOWN

Next morning Wishy Washy decided that on the following day she'd make one of her occasional trips to town to buy some things. She would take the donkey and cart as there would be too much for her to carry on foot. Today she had to check over the cart and harness, as well as her donkey, Dido, to be sure all was well for the trip.

But first, she had to send off her letter to Sue and Sam. As usual she summoned Sugarplum, and gave him the note she'd written the day before. Sugarplum found the dolls at the same cedar grove along the stream. Tuned in with her scene stone, Wishy Washy heard a faint tap-tapping noise from Sue and Sam's camp, a noise something like that which the woodpecker makes, yet different. As Sugarplum settled on a low curving cedar branch, Wishy Washy saw the two dolls working intently near their small fire.

Sue held one of their nails, the slightly bent one. She put it on the fire, and left it there until it glowed red. Then, wrapping leaves around the hot metal near the head she laid the nail across a stone, and Sam pounded on it with another stone which he raised over head with both hands and brought down forcefully on the nail, in just the way he had cracked nuts.

Little by little, with frequent heating, blowing on the fire, and making sparks with more pounding, the nail became flat. Listening closely, Wishy Washy could hear the small voices, "Let it get hotter, Sue" "Try to pound more down at this end, Sam" "Put some more wood on the fire" and finally "I think it's done" "We have to polish it with rocks and sand, and make a sharp edge by rubbing it on a rock" "And make a case for it."

It was plain to Wishy Washy when the new blade had been quenched in the stream and Sam used it to chop through a branch, that the dolls had made a machete, a large (doll size) chopping knife. Wishy Washy had one in her size for herself and found it extremely useful for cutting paths through the brush, peeling bark, cutting small firewood and trimming branches.

"What a useful tool for the dolls to have made!" thought the witch, "and they discovered metal work all by themselves, what clever dolls!"

Sugarplum, now growing impatient, glided from his perch, swooped low over the dolls and dropped the letter in Sue's lap. He beat the air with his wings, rose steeply between and over the great cedars and headed for his own part of the woods.

Wishy Washy turned off her screen, thought about the dolls for a bit, then went out to clean and trim Dido's hooves for the next day's trip. She also decided to wash the cart (with wishing well water, of course) and to oil the wheels.

She also had to pull up some money from the well and dry it. There was a circular wire screen that lay on the bottom of the well to catch money, and which could be cranked up on a slender chain. Wishy Washy could collect whatever wish offerings there were this way, and also clean anything out of the well that shouldn't have fallen in. Long ago Wishy Washy had rescued a drowning kitten this way.

Her shopping list was on her mind, sugar (for better pies), salt, matches, roof nails, flour, thread, rice, new stove pipe, oats, dog food, library books, chocolate, baking soda, soap. And then she had to think about what to wear.

To Sue and Sam the arrival of the letter was another major, incomprehensible happening in their lives.

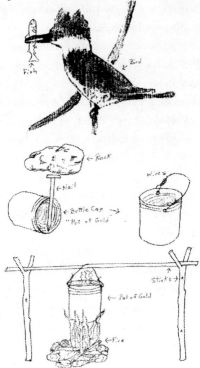

They studied the picture of the kingfisher, and saw that there was something in its beak. They recognized that it represented a bird something like a jay and something like a woodpecker, but different from both, with a large strong bill, blue-grey body, and a white collar.

Sam said, "I think I saw one of those, where the stream spreads out, near the place the pot of gold came from."

Sue said, "We should watch for it again, because its picture is here. What about the other picture?"

Sam took this in quickly. He reached for the pot and the remaining straight nail. While Sue held it against the inside top edge of the pot, he struck the head of the nail with a stone to make a hole in the pot. Turning the pot to the opposite side the dolls punched a second hole. After they figured out the properties of the wire that bound the letter, Sue slipped it through the holes and twisted the ends so that it made a neat, fireproof handle.

That evening Sue and Sam hung their pot over the fire, and with water, berries and ground hazel nuts, they cooked their first meal in it.

Berries and nuts were growing scarce close by the dolls' camp. For this reason as well as to look for the kingfisher, Sue and Sam decided to move downstream on the following day.

Night came, with owl hoots and the passing of a family of raccoons near by Sue and Sam's camp. The shredded shell of a crayfish lay on the streambank in the morning. Sue and Sam, of course, being just pieces of wood, alarmed no wildlife by their presence.

The dolls gathered their moveable possessions; stone axes, machete, and Sue's headband. Wishy Washy's letters were rolled in a tight bundle around the remaining nail. Finally they put glowing coals covered with ashes in their pot of gold and took their fire with them. They left behind their lean-to, berry carrier and a few nut shells and stones.

They moved downstream with some difficulty for

though it was a time of low water, the stream bed was full of slippery stones and tangles of logs and roots where there wasn't water. However, by late morning the dolls arrived at the sandbank where the old bottle lay half buried. Another stream joined theirs here, and formed a pool even in this low water season.

Sue and Sam decided to stop and camp here, hoping they would see the kingfisher again. The upper stream banks were full of rodent burrows and obviously were densely inhabited. A tiny beach bordering the pool offered a camping spot for Sue and Sam. They dropped their loads here, and made a new campfire.

Sam said, "I'm hungry. Let's look for food now and build a roof later. I'll take the pot so we can carry something back."

"Let's bring an axe and the machete too," said Sue.

They climbed up the stream bank and entered the woods to look for berries and nuts. They blazed a trail, chopping occasional marks on stems and branches so that they could find their way back to their camp. Sam wore the pot over his head to leave his hands free.

Soon they heard a great deal of noise, cracking, crashing, growling, roaring, buzzing and slurping. Sue and Sam climbed up a branch to observe a bear attacking a bee tree. He tore out slabs of rotting wood until he could plunge his paws inside the tree and pull out masses of comb and honey. A cloud of angry bees attacked his face. When the black bear had had enough he shuffled off.

Sue and Sam wondered what he was eating and made their way to the tree. There was plenty of scattered comb and honey on the ground, and since the bees could not sting the wooden dolls, Sue and Sam quickly discovered the delight of the delicious sweet honey and ate their fill. They loaded up their pot with all it could hold and returned to their new camp in time to erect a roof before evening.

As the morning sun revealed the stream and its banks

beneath the tall trees and melted away an enshrouding mist, Sue and Sam stirred after their night's sleep.

Soon Sue noticed an unfamiliar birdcall, and following it with her ears and eyes, spotted a blue-grey bird on a limb overhanging the pool. Suddenly it flew over the water, hung hovering an instant, then plunged headfirst into the pool. Without hesitation it was back on the wing to return to perch on the limb, with something wriggling in its beak.

The bird quickly swallowed its catch, then repeated the same performance three more times. The two dolls were curious as to what the kingfisher was catching and eating with such relish.

After a quick breakfast of honey with a few berries and seeds, Sue and Sam put some slow burning sticks on the fire, and went down to the edge of the pool. They saw lots of shiny, swimming shapes in the water. Sue and Sam waded in and tried to catch some of these fish, and failed. The fish either kept their distance, or if Sue or Sam managed to grab at one with their hands, they found it too strong and slippery to grip.

"What we need," said Sam, "is something like that bird's beak." Sam waded out of the water and went to look for a stick. Sue left the water too and sat back to rest in a mossy spot. She watched Sam as he returned to the streamside with a piece of huckleberry branch, straight and as long as he was tall. With the nail machete, he formed a sharp point on one end of the stick. Presently the two waded into the pool again, watched critically by the kingfisher from a branch overhead. Sam thrust again and again at flashing forms in the water. At last he struck something solid and his spear became alive in his hands. The two dolls struggled to drag the flopping fish ashore, for though it was a small fish that the kingfisher could swallow easily, Sue and Sam were small dolls, and this their first catch. At last they managed to drag the fish up the beach, where it quickly died from the spear wound in its heart.

Now Sue and Sam had never eaten fish or meat before, but they didn't have any reason not to like it. They cut the fish into pieces and tried some. Both thought it was delicious. After eating several pieces each, Sue tried roasting some on a stick over the fire. Both dolls decided that this was so much better that they would cook all the rest of their fish. But not now. Both dolls were ready for a nap.

Meanwhile the Wishy Washy Witch had found her clothes for town. She hitched Dido between the two wooden shafts at the front of the cart. The flowers painted on the sides of the cart shown up beautifully now that the cart was freshly washed.

Next she spoke to Marley, and her special goat-dog, Bisquit, and told them that they had to stay home and be in charge of the two goats. The goats, Ahmed and Patina, were lectured to also, for what good it did. They would stay home, but would get into whatever mischief they could find. Once they had pulled the clothes off Wishy Washy's clothes line.

She put a water bucket in the cart, a jug of wishing well water for herself, a lunch and a basket of mushrooms she had picked in the woods. She climbed up on the seat and switched a branch over Dido's head, saying "giddy-up Dido" and clucking her tongue. They proceeded at an ambling walk while Dido browsed on tufts of grass and berry bushes along the way. Down her lane, Witch Way, on to the road, Which Way, with two miles to go to town.

As Dido was nosing in some low berry bushes, three grouse burst out from cover beating their wings frantically and flying off in different directions. Maybe Dido was really startled by the birds, or maybe it was just an excuse for some donkey fun, but he tore off at a gallop, braying at the top of his voice. The cart with Wishy Washy holding on with both hands, bounced along behind.

Dido didn't stop running until he had scattered the people and dogs from the center of town and drew up in a cloud of dust in front of the library where he started munching some decorative shrubbery. For Wishy Washy, it was not unusual to have trouble controlling the donkey on these trips. She accepted her safe but quick arrival as all for the best.

It was still half an hour early for the Post Office or Library to be open, though a few children were to be seen outside the small school next door. She adjusted her hat and waved to the children as if she were accepting applause for a stage act.

Wishy Washy decided to move Dido to where she could tie him to a nearby tree and she filled his water bucket from a public faucet. She would walk across the road and make all her purchases at the general store and then go to the Post Office and Library before setting off for home.

The people in town knew Wishy Washy well, but did not know of the special abilities she had with her scene screen and her friend Sugarplum, nor did they know about Sue and Sam. They were used to sharing gossip with her as the Wishing Well lady, and she was in turn the subject of some gossip and speculation. Wishy Washy entered the general store and began gathering her purchases. When she, with the help of the store clerk, Mr. Armstrong, had completed her list, she paid for the purchases. Besides the items on her list, Wishy Washy got a bag of licorice to share with Dido on the way home. She also found a treat for each of the other animals waiting for her there.

The bell on the door of the store tinkled as Dwayne Trudger entered. "Hi Wishy Washy," he said, "How are things? Going well I hope! Ha ha," he laughed, giving her a wink. "Can I help you carry these things out?"

"Oh please yes!" said Wishy Washy, "Dido and the cart are just across the road."

"I saw them," said Dwayne.

The two carried armloads across to the cart, where they

found Dido happily munching apples from the back of a very old pick-up truck that was now parked next to him.

"This truck belongs to Dora Dinghy, doesn't it?" asked Wishy Washy.

"Oh, yes," said Dwayne, "I just saw her go into the library."

"I'll just leave her this bag of mushrooms inside the truck; they're worth more than the apples Dido can eat," said Wishy Washy. She dropped a bag of mushrooms in through a broken side window of the truck.

"I see you're getting new stove pipe," said Dwayne. "It reminds me that I have something at my shop to show you. Can you come in on your way home?"

"Well . . . I hadn't intended . . .," said Wishy Washy, then she smiled and said, "but if Dido takes me there, and stops there when I tell him, I'll come in." Actually she was curious to see what might be new in Dwayne's second hand shop "Trudger's Treasures" on the edge of town.

She thanked Dwayne for his help and went into the Post Office.

Wishy Washy had a letter from an old school friend in her box, as well as a promotional copy of *GLAMOUR GOAT* magazine, and an advertisement for insurance. She thought of having a chat with the post mistress about insurance, but let it go because time was passing and she was far from home.

Wishy Washy's next stop was the Library next door. She returned a cook book, and when she spoke to Dora Dinghy, the librarian, she found that the two books she had ordered were there for her, one on bird's nests and one on washing machine repair. She checked out the books from Dora and exchanged some small talk.

Dora said, whispering from long library habit, "I knew your books were due today and that you'd be in so I brought a big bunch of bean and pea vines I pulled out of my garden. They're for your animals. I put them out in back.."

Wishy Washy didn't mention that Dido had eaten the

ornamental plantings out front, nor the apples. Wishy Washy picked up the bundle of vines when she left and put them in the cart.

Her business finished, Wishy Washy gave Dido a piece of licorice as she untied him, took one for herself, picked up the water bucket, and clambered up on to the cart seat. Dido seemed agreeable to going home, so they plodded out of town, Dido curling his lip at a tethered saddle horse, and Wishy Washy waving at Tony Armstrong.

The stove pipe sections and water bucket clanked together with every small bump in the road. Soon they reached "Trudger's Treasures" with its sign, hand made of sheet metal, showing a pirate with a parrot and a treasure chest. The building had once been a barn, and in the yard in back lay several old vehicles and pieces of logging and farming equipment, windmills, waterpumps and old iron stoves.

Wishy Washy brought Dido to a halt, climbed down and tied him to a large salmon colored concrete sculpture of a pig with a ring in its nose. Thick dark clouds were approaching from the north, so Wishy Washy told herself, "I must not delay here, I'll just go in for a few minutes."

Wishy Washy entered the shop, where a wealth of objects, some utilitarian, some artistic, some neither, covered tables and much of the floor space. Shelves hung from above. Dwayne Trudger greeted Wishy Washy affably. "I'm glad you could come in," he said, "I guess Dido must be behaving himself today." Wishy Washy gave a smile and a nod to that, and Dwayne went on, "I made this stove pipe ornament I thought you ought to see."

He pointed to a sheet metal bird with a long bill on a round base. It would slip right over the top of the stove pipe and keep rain from entering. Dwayne demonstrated how it would rotate to always face into the wind. The bird's eye was a marble set in a hole in the metal so light came through it from both sides. Wishy Washy agreed to buy it and took a quick look through the rest of the store. Hanging on a rack of clothes, she found a black jacket with a painted parrot on the back that she liked very much. She decided to take the jacket too.

After paying Dwayne, Wishy Washy quickly excused herself, saying that it looked like rain. She put her metal bird and jacket in the cart, and looking around, saw that the clouds were advancing southward.

She got up on the cart and started Dido on his way. She wanted to urge him to hurry, yet was afraid he might hurry too fast and bounce her out of the cart or tip it over. But it went well, Dido clopped along at a fast walk. Before long they again came to the sign marking where Witch Way turned off from Which Way. A little further on and they were home.

The dogs jumped joyfully against the sides of the cart, and the goats crowded round to see if there was something to eat. Ahmed snatched at the bundle of pea and bean vines from Dora and dragged them half out of the cart.

Wishy Washy said "What good animals you all were! See what I've brought for you" and she distributed the rest of the treats to all the animals.

She unhitched Dido and put him away with a bowl of oats. The same for the goats in their goat house. Wishy Washy brought all the things into her house that she had bought, and just in time, as the first raindrops were starting to fall.

X

THE CROW'S NEST

The next morning Wishy Washy put up some dill pickles in jars; she had some cucumbers that had to be used.

As she was finishing that job, and putting lids on her jars, she was thinking of Sue and Sam. She wondered how they were doing at learning to catch and eat fish. She also wanted to encourage them to move downstream and reach the lake shore where she'd have a chance of finding them.

Therefore she watched for a foraging Stellar jay, and when one happened along, working its way through the fir trees, she sent out a call for Sugarplum. Once again, after little more than an hour he arrived.

In the meantime Wishy Washy had prepared another

letter to the dolls. This one showed them how to make a fish trap in shallow water by placing stones in rows on the bottom of the stream so that they made a funnel shaped entrance leading into a small pen where fish could easily be speared or caught by hand. Wishy Washy drew a picture of Sue and Sam lifting and carrying stones in the stream and of the stones laid out into the trap shape with fish coming in.

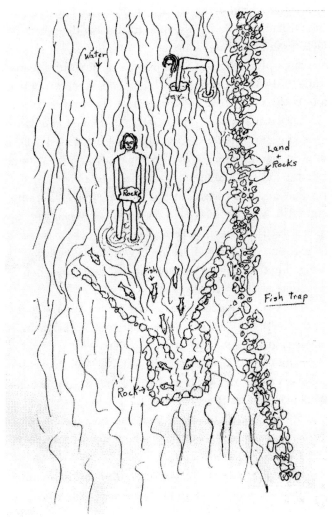

She decided this was enough of a message for today. Wishy Washy sent Sugarplum off with the rolled letter and reached for her "scene stone."

The rain from the night before left the trees still dripping, but as the morning wore on the sun shone and started to dry branches and undergrowth. Sue and Sam had been trying to spear another fish, but so far had not succeeded. Sugarplum found them standing in the water, Sue trying to shoo fish towards Sam who would try to spear them, but the targets were quick and agile.

Sugarplum alighted on a branch to survey the scene, while Wishy Washy, at home with her scene screen, watched too. Besides the dolls, she saw the tiny lean-to with its fireplace, a wisp of smoke rising from it. All seemed well. However, the continually thickening carpet of fallen leaves showed that summer was over. Wishy Washy hoped that her fish trap letter would help Sue and Sam to survive.

Sue and Sam waded out of the stream to rest, still without a fish. Sam sat down and began to resharpen the fish spear which had been dulled against the rocks by missing thrusts. Sue went to tend the fire. Sugarplum flew down between them, dropped the letter and squawked once before returning to his previous perch.

The dolls dropped what they were doing and ran to the letter. The two studied the pictures and soon it was apparent that they grasped the idea of the fish trap.

"This seems like a good idea," said Sam. "See, like in the picture, we put rocks in rows to make the fish get into this small place," he said, pointing to the trap in the picture.

"But the water is too deep here," said Sue. "Let's look on further down the stream and see if there is a place where it is more wide and shallow."

The dolls made preparations for an exploratory walk. Sam put the pot of gold on his head and took up the machete in its case. Sue had an ax in her belt. Both dolls were hungry and hoped to find something to eat along the way.

Sugarplum flew off to his own part of the woods at this time, and Wishy Washy too, had to go about other business.

The dolls started walking downstream. Some places were easy, at other places they had to climb over obstacles or avoid them by wading around in the stream.

They came to where a bush of red huckleberries hung low beside the stream. These berries looked like beautiful red jewels, and stayed on the bush late into the year. Sue and Sam each gathered an armful and sat in a sandy spot to eat.

From a high fir limb two other pairs of eyes watched them. It was a pair of crows. Crows like to decorate their nests with interesting trinkets, such as shells, bones, and colorful stones. As years go by, the nests became more and more elaborate. The crow couple watching Sue and Sam had sent their latest brood out of the nest to join the crow flock. Now they were making some repairs and decorations before winter set in.

Together they dived from their perch to land on the sand next to Sue and Sam. Sue offered them some berries, thinking they might be friends of Sugarplum's. With that, one crow seized Sue around the waist in its beak. The other grabbed Sam, and the crows easily flew off with these light burdens.

Higher and higher they circled, until they reached the level of their nest built on the limb of a tall fir tree. The crows landed with the petrified dolls. They set to work pulling and pushing to weave the arms and legs of the two dolls into the twiggy structure of the nest. Finally, the crows stood back at the edges of the nest to admire their work, then, with a few squawks and caws, flew off to find a meal.

Presently Sue and Sam grew less paralyzed with terror. They found themselves so well built into the nest structure that at first they could hardly move. With much wiggling Sam eventually freed one arm. With it he was able to reach his machete and slash some strands of bark and limber twigs that held the rest of his body in place. Sue also was starting to wiggle herself free. Sam was finally able to crawl out onto the center of the nest, and from there he went to help Sue get free.

Disentangled from the nest, the two looked around them. They were frighteningly high. The tops of other big trees could be seen just below and around them. They watched a squirrel in a fir top next to them cut a late fir cone and drop it far, far down to the ground to be gathered later.

Looking in another direction, they could see over the tops of lower trees that stood in the small valley where their stream ran. They could trace the path of the downhill flowing water off into the distance. There they saw that it met a large body of water, the largest they had ever seen. This was the lake that lay not far from the home of the Wishy Washy Witch.

Sue said to Sam, "Oh, Sam, let's go to that big water! I bet there'll be more fish and maybe other things to eat. Some places berries are hard to find now that the leaves are falling and it's getting cold."

Sam replied, "We have to get back down to the ground before we go anywhere, and we'd better do it before the crows come back."

They looked over the edge of the nest and through the clutter of twigs that formed it. Never had they been so high before. The tree that held the nest was too steep and smooth for them to climb down. The limbs were too far apart for them to climb from one to the other and in fact, the lower half of the tree had no limbs. Even if the two could climb, clinging to the bark of the trunk like squirrels, they would be exhausted long before they reached the bottom. Sue and Sam moved to another side of the nest and looked down. Here they could see that another tree had partly fallen over, and leaned against the tree they were on. The two trees touched several feet below the nest.

Sue said, "Sam, if we could get down to that leaning tree, it would be much easier to climb down than this tree we're on."

"You're right," said Sam, "but how can we climb down to it?"

The two looked over the nest for ideas. It was made of twigs, interlaced with grass and natural fibers such as cedar bark. Decorations included the wishbone of some bird, some feathers, some pebbles and a squirrel's skull.

Sam said, "With these sticks and strips of bark we could make a ladder except there aren't enough sticks to make one long enough to reach the leaning tree and it would be too heavy."

"But", said Sue, "we don't need a whole ladder like we would if we were going up. All we need is a single pole to slide all the way down to the leaning tree. We have only to go from this nest to a limb, lower the pole, and slide down to the next limb."

Sue and Sam set to work pulling the longest twigs out of the nest and making a pile, and another tangle of fibers including strips of cedar bark. Then they lashed sticks together end to end. After they'd connected several in this way, their pole was almost too long to handle. The two working together lowered it over the side of the nest and toward a large limb below. When they were hanging their pole full length it still didn't reach the limb.

"Hold it Sam," said Sue, "I'll get another stick."

Sam struggled to support the heavy poles while Sue got another piece and lashed it to the end. They eased the pole down until its bottom rested on top of a big limb. The top of their pole they attached loosely to the nest so that it would not slip but so that they could free it by pulling from below.

Making sure they still had their tools and pot of gold,

Sue, and then Sam climbed out of the nest and onto the wiggly pole. Every joint they had lashed wiggled as they gripped the pole with arms and legs and slid down. It was scary!

Soon they were both standing on the big limb. They lowered the pole again to another big limb and so on until they reached the leaning tree. This was more like going downhill than down a cliff.

In a few spots where the bark was smooth, Sue and Sam chopped footholds and hand holds in the bark for safety, though most of the way it wasn't necessary.

As the sun was setting they descended the rest of the distance in deep shadow, to the ground. They found their way along the creek to their lean-to with the last of the light, as the chilling air became a mist filling the valley. Sue and Sam managed to revive their still smoldering fire and collapse on their beds in exhaustion.

XI

FISHING

Daylight came wrapped in a heavy ground fog. Sue and Sam arose and crouched by their fire. They had learned to make tea of streamside herbs like mint, which they had with a bit of remaining honey stored in a hazel nut shell. They used hazel shells also for cups. There was no other food left. The two had planned to try the fish trap here, but now were afraid that the pair of crows would come back to reclaim them when the fog had lifted.

Over their tea, Sue and Sam decided to move on further downstream and look for another place where kingfishers were fishing.

They packed up their few possessions. By now they had

lost all but the latest letter from the Wishy Washy Witch with the fish trap diagram on it.

Stealthily they moved off downstream again, hidden by the fog from sharp eyed lookouts in the crows' nest above. They carried hot embers from their fire in the pot of gold, and left behind only their small lean-to.

Once again, their way was difficult in places with many large, slippery stones and tangles of twigs and vines to get through. Other stretches were easy crossings of sand or gravel beaches.

Up ahead, a fallen cedar trunk made a natural dam which formed a pool of clear water. Sue and Sam could see tiny fish swimming there, and so could the kingfisher perched on an overhanging limb. The bird was waiting for larger fish than those which attracted the two dolls.

One side of the pool was shallow water, which gradually increased in depth towards the other side and the log dam.

Sam said, "This looks like a good place. Let's make a fish trap here first, and then set up our camp while the trap collects fish."

Sue unrolled the diagram for the trap, and both dolls looked at it. "Suppose I start here, on the shore, laying stones, and Sam, you go out there in the deeper water and start laying stones for the other side of the trap opening."

And so they proceeded wading and carrying stones large enough to lie on the bottom yet reach to the surface. As they worked they got closer together since it was a funnel shaped opening they were making. They completed that and the enclosed pen which would hold the fish led into it by the spreading side of the "funnel". They collected a few more stones to have ready to close the entrance of the pen when fish were inside.

Sue and Sam were ready for a brief rest and warming in a sunny spot. Next they found a place for their camp, built their fire and constructed a lean-to.

"I'm really getting hungry for some fish, Sue," said Sam, when the camp was made.

"Let's check the trap now," she replied, and Sam had only to grab his fish spear and they were ready.

At the trap they saw that a few little fish had gone into the pen as they hoped, but that a large school of fish was moving back and forth near the entrance to the funnel.

Sam said, "Sue, why don't you go upstream of those fish and chase them down into the trap, and I'll stay here to block the entrance to the pen with rocks."

And so Sue, finding a stick to beat the water with, moved to the right place and waded into the water. She waded towards the fish, beating the surface. The fish were frightened. Some found their way around the end of the funnel arm and escaped the trap. Some found places to slither between the stones forming the funnel and escaped that way.

As Sue moved down towards Sam at the pen, a number of fish dashed ahead of her through the funnel entrance into the pen.

"Now!" both dolls said together as they began to pile stones across the entrance to the pen. The entrance closed, Sue and Sam found a wildly struggling mass of fish in the pen. As they watched, a larger one leaped in the air and escaped over the side of the pen, and small ones were trying to wriggle between the stones. Sam waded in and repeatedly thrust his spear into the water. By having previously used the fish spear for roasting pieces of fish over the fire, Sam had hardened its wooden point so now it was more durable.

The struggles of the fish stirred up the mud on the bottom. The water grew cloudy, the flashing forms were hard to see. But three times Sam was successful and had a fish on his spear for Sue and him to struggle with and subdue. After the third fish Sam scored no more hits and soon it seemed all the rest of the fish had found their way out of the trap.

Sue said, "Well, the trap works, but it's not easy." In fact, each fish would feed the two dolls for more than a day.

Sue and Sam pushed the spear through the gills of each fish so that all three hung from the middle of it. Then each doll lifted an end of the spear, and though it bent under the weight, they were able to carry their catch to the lean-to and fire.

Now it was time to eat! They cut up and roasted fish and ate until they were full.

Sam sat by the fire playing with a hazel twig and a strip of cedar bark. He had started to make a device to hang the remaining fish in the smoke of the fire to preserve them, but before he finished, Sue had solved the problem herself. She suspended the fish from a stick laid on two forked uprights.

Sam continued playing with the bark and twig anyway. He tied the bark to one end of the twig, bent the twig under his leg, and tied the bark to the other end, making a bow. He plucked the string of bark with a finger. It gave out a low hum. He held the bow in his teeth, and strumming the string gave another sound.

Sam tried holding the bow against different objects; a rock, the pot of gold, a hazel nut shell, each trial giving a different sound when the string was plucked. Soon Sue and Sam were singing along with the bow string. They made a song about fishing, with not many words, but lots of versions of the kingfisher's cry by both string and voice.

Finally Sue and Sam slept. The night was not foggy. A light wind from the south sent high clouds scudding across the face of the moon, casting weird moving shadows through the forest, accompanied now by owl hoots.

XII

ON TO THE LAKE

The next day dawned with a light rain pattering on the lean-to. The rain increased in the late morning and continued most of the day.

Sue and Sam stayed in the lean-to. There were plenty of twigs and old cones protected under the thatching foliage of a nearby cedar to provide dry firewood. Sam brought some to make a woodpile at the low end of the lean-to. The remaining fish hung in the smoke of the tiny fire.

While the rain kept Sue and Sam in, the pair were ready for a day of rest. They had been through many struggles and adventures. It felt good to just sleep late and think and talk about things.

Sue said to Sam: "Look how high the water is getting!" and indeed, through the rain, Sam could see the stream had grown and its waterline had risen. It was a long way from reaching the camp, but it was definitely a much bigger stream.

Sam said, "I can't see our fish trap, the water must cover all the stones now."

"Yes," said Sue, "and from the looks of that strong current, I think it could even roll the stones away. All this water must go on to that really big water we saw from the crows' nest. Do you think it's far from here, Sam?"

"I don't think so. Shall we go there?"

"Not now, but if the rain has stopped tomorrow let's go and see it!"

"Yes," said Sam, "the fishing might be easier there, and there's no reason to stay here. We might as well see the world."

That plan made, Sue and Sam ate some smoked fish. Then they sang some more songs accompanied by the bow. Later they lay back in their moss beds to doze and listen to the rain.

Before dark the rain stopped, and only the rushing stream and dripping trees could be heard. Sue and Sam walked out to the stream's edge and marveled at the volume and force of the moving water. They looked downstream and wondered what sort of way they would be able to find along the side of the swollen stream in the morning.

The moon rose, and once again it could be glimpsed through openings in the wind-driven clouds. A breeze brushed the tops of the tall trees. Sue and Sam replenished their fire and returned to their beds.

The next morning the sun shone from among only a few clouds. Sue and Sam ate, then packed up their few belongings to carry with them. Once again, hot coals from the fire went into the pot of gold, which they would take turns carrying. Otherwise, their tools hung on their bodies and they had nothing else. Sam decided to leave his bow behind in the lean-to. It would be easy to make another the next time they wanted to sing.

As they started off, Sue said, "Look, the stream has already fallen." It was easy to see the stretch along each side of the stream that had recently been under fast moving water. Much of it was swept clean, but there were places where entangling roots had caught and held the moss, branches, bits of bark and vines that were carried along by the stream. These piles made difficult obstacles for the two dolls to climb over and through. They boosted and pulled each other over logs and large stones.

Eventually the stream grew broader and slower. Sue and Sam were forced away from the water by a cat-tail marsh. The cat-tails and shallow water were so difficult to traverse that it was easier to move under the low bushes on one side. Passing through the bushes, and then through some tall grass, they stopped and looked. "We're here," said Sue.

"It's really big," said Sam.

They were at the lakeshore. They could see more tall trees on the distant shore, but even so, the sparkling stretch of water seemed to mark the edge of the world.

The shoreline was marsh in some places, but also beach and high bank. Accumulations of driftwood lay here and there. Sue and Sam selected a spot close to the woods for their camp.

They quickly made a lean-to, built their fire and gathered some moss for bedding. Their camp was made.

The two were eager to explore the lake shore. Never before had they been able to see so much sky. As the clouds thinned, the lakeshore was flooded with sunshine. Back on their forest stream, Sue and Sam had seen only small patches of sunshine. Now they were out of that shady, green world and into one flooded with light.

All at once a great noise came from the water. Sue and Sam ran to a small willow bush overhanging the lake and peered between its branches. A large gathering of ducks had been disturbed by the arrival of a pair of new ducks. All were quacking at the top of their lungs.

There were so many new things for Sue and Sam to see. Where a patch of long grass grew to the water's edge, a busy muskrat cut a mouthful of stems and swam off with it. At a distance, they watched a fox hunting mice in the long grass.

Sue and Sam moved along a stretch of narrow sandy beach, lapped by wavelets. Now and then their feet were wet by the lapping water but that was no concern.

Sam said, "I don't see any fish."

Sue replied, "There's so much water, they're probably out where it's deeper."

"Well," said Sam, "we'll have to find some way to catch them."

Soon they came to where a patch of cattails were growing in shallow water. It was a strange, forest-like place. Sam startled a frog that was floating in a patch of sunlight at the edge of the cattails. It plunged to deeper water, startling Sam.

The pair saw a dragonfly hovering low over the water, then they saw several more. One of the beautiful, large insects landed on a cattail stem right above Sue's head and they were able to get a close look at it.

There were so many wonders of nature that were new to Sue and Sam. A short ways away from shore floated water lilies, their leaves lying flat on the surface. While looking at the lilies, Sue happened to gaze into the clear water, and saw under the lily pad the face of a large fish looking up at her. The wide mouth of this fish could easily swallow Sue and Sam too!

She said, "Sam, look, I didn't know fish could get so large!" Sam added, "we'd better be careful in this new place."

The two strolled back along the lakeshore toward their camp. They watched a heron, standing in shallow water on its long legs as it speared a fish with its long, pointed beak.

Though dragonflies and water lilies still were present,

signs of autumn were everywhere. The leaves of the willows near the shore were turning yellow and starting to fall, likewise those of the alders at the edge of the woods. The long grass near the lakeshore was starting to yellow too.

Back at the camp Sue and Sam decided to make a second fish spear and for both of them to try their luck. They hadn't found a good place yet for the fish trap. For reassurance, they saw a kingfisher plunge from his perch on a dead limb into the lake to appear with a wriggling minnow and fly back to his spot.

They found a place where a large willow limb had fallen down to float on the lake's surface, while it was still rooted to shore. The two dolls climbed out along this limb and looked for fish. At first they mainly saw their own reflections, but soon found that there were places shaded from the sky where they could see into the water.

After not too long, a school of minnows, moving along the shore, started to swim under the limb. Quick as a flash, Sue's spear plunged in like the heron's beak and she had one! The rest of the minnows disappeared instantly. Sue and Sam agreed that they were tired, and with the sun going down, they took their fish back to camp.

XIII

HAPPENINGS AT THE LAKE

That evening, while sitting by their fire, Sue began to sing some more, and included some duck quacking, which Sam thought was very funny.

"I'm going to make a new bow," said Sam, "and play it along with you."

Earlier in the day, Sam had found a particularly springy twig, from a yew tree, among the other pieces of lakeside driftwood. He'd set it aside for making his bow.

With the machete, he carved some notches in the ends, and with Sue's help he was able to bend and string it with a tough stringy cedar root, with a loop tied in each end. When he had it completed, the two dolls sang several new songs.

Sam tried various different ways of plucking the bow to get different sounds.

While he was trying to pluck the string with a grass stem, it slipped from his fingers and shot out into the darkness. Intrigued by this effect, Sam tried deliberately shooting another grass stem. This time it pierced a leaf which was part of the lean-to roof and likewise was lost in the darkness.

After a few more tries, Sam laid the bow aside and the two dolls slept. The night was clear and chilly; a dense mist covered the lake and its shores by morning.

Sue and Sam sat by their fire in the grey dawn. They drank tea made from the mint that grew near the lake. They decided to explore along the lakeshore where they hadn't gone the day before. Sam said that he thought his new bow might work in combination with his fish spear to better his chances. Presently the rising sun began to clear the mist, and Sue and Sam went out on their walk.

They had not gone far when Sue said, "Look, here is a shallow place."

Indeed a stretch of shallow, gravelly bottom connected a large off-shore rock to land. Sue and Sam could wade across it. It was a perfect spot for a fish trap. The two dolls set to work moving stones, and soon had made a much larger trap than their previous one. They went back to their lean to for lunch, and to keep the fire alive. On the way, Sam plucked grass stems and shot them at leaf targets as they walked.

Sue and Sam took some time to rest from the heavy work they had done moving stones. After about an hour the dolls took up fish spears and the bow, and went to see if they had caught any fish in their trap.

"Oh look," moaned Sue, "he's getting them all!"

There stood a tall heron in the shallow water eating the fish out of the trap!

"Those are ours!" shouted Sam, "go away," and he waved his spear at the heron. The bird took little notice of the puny antics.

"What if he chases us?" said Sue.

"Look, here is some kind of rodent burrow. We can crawl in there if he comes for us," replied Sam, bravely. "Help me find some arrows and I'll chase him away."

The two dolls gathered a bundle of grass stem arrows. Then they walked to the edge of the lake, where the feeding heron towered over them like a tree. Sue carried the arrows to pass them to Sam who started shooting. The first two shots were misses, the third hit the heron on the face. It blinked and looked puzzled. A few more shots from Sam, and the big bird gradually realized where the irritation was coming from.

The heron charged at the dolls through the shallow water. With wings and beak raised it ran at the dolls making splashing footsteps all the way. Sue and Sam turned to run for the rodent burrow. At that moment Sugarplum arrived and landed at the top of a lakeside willow.

Through these passing days of early autumn the Wishy Washy Witch had continued making her preparations for winter. She brought in loads of firewood. She repaired a leak in her roof. She removed her rusty old stove pipe and replaced it with new pipe topped with the bird ornament from "Trudger's Treasures" that turned back and forth in the wind.

Now Wishy Washy took time to think of Sue and Sam again. Had they reached the lake? Was their fish trap successful? So, when she went out walking with her dogs and goats, she said to herself that she was "jay-walking," looking for a jay to get a message to Sugarplum. This she did and about mid-day Sugarplum arrived and perched on the well gate. He gave a squawk and alerted Wishy Washy, who had been hanging laundry out to dry. The witch gave the jay instructions to look for Sue and Sam, in the stream valley and along the lake shore. As he flew off, Wishy Washy turned on her scene screen and made the search through Sugarplum's eyes.

Sugarplum went to the stream where he had last seen Sue

and Sam. There was an abandoned lean-to and a cold fireplace. Sugarplum moved on, alighting on a bush or limb now and then to look around. He reached the lake, and since Sue and Sam had not moved far from the stream's mouth during their time there, the jay soon found their camp. He noticed too, the squawk and splashing of the heron, and flew to investigate.

It was with alarm that the Wishy Washy Witch and Sugarplum took in the event that was happening. Sue and Sam dashed through shallow water and grass toward the burrow, under a log, while the fierce grey-blue bird chased them on his long legs, making lunges with his beak.

The two dolls reached the burrow just inches ahead of the heron and tumbled inside. After the two had caught their breath, Sam moved closer to the burrow entrance and looked out. He saw the heron looking in. Sam shot the grass stem arrows that he still had at the furious fowl. Soon the big bird flapped its wings and flew off to a distant fir tree. We don't know whether Sam's arrows, or just the fact that there were no fish left in the trap finally drove the heron away.

Sugarplum watched as Sue and Sam emerged from the burrow and went to look at the fish trap. Two small fish remained, smaller than the heron would bother with. All the rest had been eaten by the bird or had escaped the trap. Since Sue and Sam were small, the two fish were just enough for them. They speared them out of the trap and the two dolls carried the fish off to their lean-to.

Having seen enough, the Wishy Washy Witch called Sugarplum back to her and turned off her scene screen. By the time the jay returned, the Wishy Washy Witch was already at work with pen and paper on another message to Sue and Sam.

Wishy Washy knew that Sue and Sam were at the mouth of one of the several small creeks that flowed into the lake near her house, and that if she just walked along the lakeshore crossing the tributary streams on her way, she would be likely to find the dolls' camp.

She realized, though, that this might take some time, and any number of things might delay her. In the meantime it was getting colder and real storms of wind, rain, or snow might come at any time. Sue's and Sam's lean-to would not stand up to such weather. Wishy Washy wanted to teach them to build a more protective shelter, in this, hopefully, her final message to them. She decided on a tepee style of building, of sticks with a covering of bark.

She drew pictures of the framework of the tepee, and of Sue and Sam peeling bark and attaching strips to the tepee with ties and sticky pitch. She drew a picture of the dolls gathering pitch from a wound in the bark of a fir tree. The final picture showed the finished tepee with Sam standing outside and Sue poking her head out the door. The smoke from the fire inside curled out the top of the tepee in her picture.

Wishy Washy had given Sugarplum a cookie to eat while she worked. He was ready then, when she rolled up her picture, to take the message and fly off with it to Sue and Sam.

XIV

AUTUMN DAYS AT THE LAKE AND THE WITCH'S HOUSE

When Sugarplum arrived at Sue's and Sam's camp with the message, it was now a welcome and familiar experience for the two dolls. They accepted the message and Sugarplum flew off to mind his jay business. It was getting on towards evening. To make a change from their fish diet, Sue and Sam had been chopping open some fir cones that a squirrel had dropped from high above, practically on their lean-to. The fir seeds were very good, but very small. It was a lot of work to get enough out of the cones for a meal. At any rate, the two dolls had fish smoking over the fire for the next day. That evening Sue and Sam played the bow and sang again for a while. Sam made up a song about Sue going fishing:

"Sue spun twine and fishing line
of thread made by a spider.
Sam stripped bark and heard a lark
as he sat there beside her.
Sue went fishing on the pond
she hoped to catch a tadpole.
She was doing really fine
until she felt her log roll.
In she plunged with pole and net
and that ended her fishing.
To lose her pole and get all wet
was not what she was wishing.
A large mouth bass he made a pass
and took in little Susie.
He spit her out cause she was wood
and he was really choosey.
Sue she came home very late
and Sam ran out to meet her.
He had hugs and honey jugs
just right there to greet her."

In fact, this fishing event never actually happened; which is just as well, since Sue and Sam had no honey left.

The night was cold, the morning was misty, and for the first time a light frost covered the ground, the grass, and trees around the lake. A thin rim of ice marked the shore. Sue and Sam marveled at the changes without understanding.

With the daylight the two dolls studied the message from the witch. It was not hard to understand. As the sun rose higher, the frost and ice disappeared. Among the branches all around the lakeshore, a myriad of spider webs, made visible by a coating of droplets from the mist, glistened in the strengthening sunshine. Sue and Sam set to work gathering long sticks for the tepee. They decided that they needed a ladder too, to build the structure and that meant more sticks. Then, they made a trip into the woods and gathered cedar bark from low-hanging branches. With the experience and tools they had developed, the job was not difficult.

They put up a tripod with the first three sticks, then leaned others against the tripod to make a circular floor. With the ladder, they tied all the sticks together at the top. Collecting and using the sticky fir pitch to fasten the cedar bark to the sides of the tepee came next.

It was a messy job, and when finished the two dolls washed in the cold lake water. They dried and warmed themselves by the fire and had some lunch. Then Sam built a new fire inside the tepee and made it a door of cedar bark. He moved his moss bed inside and lay back to enjoy the warmth, admire their work, and nap a little.

Sue went out on her own. She went to the lakeshore to enjoy the view. As she sat in a sunny spot she watched an otter surface, and swim back and forth along the shore apparently watching her. For safety's sake Sue ran to a small willow and climbed into the branches, getting herself covered with spider webs in her hurry. Soon the otter turned away and disappeared in the deep water.

Sam was awakened by Sue calling, "Sam, Sam! Come out and see me!" Sam stepped out of the tepee rubbing his eyes. He saw Sue before him, but all shiny, silky white from neck to feet. Her legs, arms and body were all covered with a fitting suit of layers of spider web!

"It's so warm," said Sue.

Sam had to try a spider web suit himself. Webs were in the bushes all around the tepee. He applied several layers to his body. When a rip occurred when he raised his arm, he easily patched it with more web. After both dolls had paraded around in their new suits, they decided that the suits were for even colder weather. They were too hot for the sunny afternoon so the dolls peeled them off and went out to explore a little more before dark.

At about that same time the Wishy Washy Witch was thinking to herself about Sue and Sam and the tepee. Would they build it that very day? Would it prove a good shelter against the increasingly cold weather? She also had to plan a trip out along the lakeshore to look for them. With this on her mind she was going about her work.

It was time to bring oats to the donkey and goats. She was filling their bowls before she realized that Dido, the donkey, was missing. His gate was broken and he was gone!

The gate was an old one. Maybe he kicked it and broke it, she thought, maybe he just leaned against it and it collapsed.

Wishy Washy shut the goats in their house with oats, and taking a rope, called her dogs, and they set out to look for Dido. At first a few fresh hoof prints pointed the way. Farther on the prints disappeared on hard ground where Witch Way met Which Way. On a guess, Wishy Washy continued on the way towards town. Now and then she thought she saw a faint donkey track. Then she came to a sandy area with many tracks and a spot where Dido obviously had scraped the ground with his hooves and rolled. He did this frequently at home. But it was starting to get dark and Wishy Washy had no light. She'd have to put off her donkey hunt until morning.

The new day started with a cloudy sky, but was warmer than the day before. When Wishy Washy awoke she remembered that Dido was out, and that she would have to find him.

She wasted no time in getting ready. Once she was dressed and fed, she took care of the other animals, and calling her dogs, she was ready to start, with a rope and a pocket full of carrots and sugar lumps. She called, "Marley, bring my stick," and Marley brought Wishy Washy her donkey stick.

They walked down the road to where Dido had rolled the day before. "Dido," she called loudly, and from far away came an answering bray. Again she called, and again the same response. Following the sound, Wishy Washy and the dogs continued down the road until they reached a path going off to the side that she had never noticed before. The braying came from that direction, and there were fresh donkey tracks on the path.

The way passed through thick woods, then led up a hill where forest had been cleared. Here she found Dido. He was pressing himself against a fence to be closer to the friendly mare on the other side. Wishy Washy offered carrots to both Dido and the mare, and then attaching her rope to Dido's halter, tried to lead him home. It was difficult to get him to leave his friend, so Wishy Washy used her sugar lumps and stick to get him started. The dogs barked and nipped at his tail. Even so, he tried to go back several times, but Wishy Washy spoke very firmly to him and finally the donkey was willing to be led along, with many stops for browsing.

Before they were halfway home, it started pouring. Then Dido was ready to hurry home. All four; two dogs, witch and donkey were soon soaked. Some sugar lumps melted in Wishy Washy's pocket. When they finally got home, wet and cold, Wishy Washy tied some poles across Dido's gateway until she could make a new gate.

The donkey had a roof over his manger, and a dry place to lie down. The goats, snug in their house, bleated a greeting. The dogs went under Wishy Washy's cabin to await their meal. Wishy Washy went in to make a fire, change her clothes and dry off. She fed the dogs. Before evening the rain stopped. Wishy Washy once again brought oats for Dido and the goats while she thought about Sue and Sam.

Wind in the night presented the new day with a layer of freshly fallen leaves, of yellows, browns and reds, and scattered small branches. It was chilly and misty in the morning, with a promise of clear skies after the sun had started its work.

For the Wishy Washy Witch, her main job of the day would have to be to build a new donkey gate.

After the usual morning chores and breakfast, Wishy Washy set out on a walk with all the animals as usual. She carried a machete and bow saw to a place she had in mind where some young fir trees had been uprooted by a spring wind storm. Their wood was dry but had not started to rot. Wishy Washy chopped off branches and sawed the poles to length. She cut a brace and three uprights. It took her three trips to carry all the pieces home. Here she bored and chiseled mortises in an upright with more than a little help from a woodpecker. The goats helped peel bark from the poles; what they did not finish Dido would do later.

Wishy Washy had fitted and nailed the gate together by time for lunch. Afterwards she hauled the heavy gate to Dido's corral and attached it to its hinges. When the job was finished and the tools put away, it was late afternoon. The low sun left cold shadows in most of the woods. It was too late to go looking for Sue and Sam that day, "but perhaps tomorrow if the weather looks right," thought Wishy Washy.

From the scene she had seen on her screen, Wishy Washy had an idea where Sue and Sam were. From the look of the lakeshore and the position of the sun at the time, she could narrow the search to the mouths of one or two streams where they entered the lake.

The shore at this side was something like the outstretched palm of a hand. Wishy Washy's home was in the space between the thumb and index finger, both of which represented streams flowing into the lake or palm of the hand. Wishy Washy believed that the two dolls were at the little finger. She hadn't been to that place for several years, but it seemed familiar on the screen. Also, she thought she would get Sugarplum to lead her along the lakeshore to the dolls. It had been impossible to do this through the thick woods earlier, but now in the more open land along the lake it should be practical. Wishy Washy could see that with all those streams to cross she had better wear her high rubber boots.

Meanwhile, Sue and Sam had repaired the damage that the heron had done to their fish trap; they hoped it wouldn't come back. They could watch the heron fishing in shallow water near the mouth of the stream. The dolls continued to catch enough fish to feed themselves, along with seeds and a few berries.

On the morning that Wishy Washy was looking for Dido, Sue and Sam were wading in the cold water repairing the fish trap. They heard a strange calling, and looked up to see a flock of geese approach the lake from the north, circle and splash down to rest from their long journey. Groups of mallards and other ducks arrived and left as well.

The fish trap was in good order before the rain began. With the first drops, Sue and Sam went to their tepee. They had collected some dry firewood and stored it under the old lean-to. With the fire built up, it was warm and comfortable in the tepee.

The dolls left the doorway uncovered so that they could look out and see the lake and the rain. The wind drove raindrops against their sturdy little shelter but could not upset it. The smoke from the fire escaped out the opening at the top of the tepee, where the poles were tied together, and disappeared in the wind.

Before dark, when the rain had stopped, the two dolls visited the fish trap again and found that they had trapped a few minnows. They waded into the cold water and speared three of them, while the rest escaped.

Sue said to Sam, "I'm glad we got these fish. We were out of food except for fir seeds."

"Yes," said Sam, "and with these three we can have a big supper and some to save.

One of them is pretty big." "I'm cold from that cold water! Let's go back to the tepee."

And so they did, and built up the fire. They even put on their spider web suits and toasted their feet in front of the fire for a while before they started cooking pieces of fish on sticks. Both Sue and Sam were ready to sleep after they were full of supper. They kept their suits on and covered up with a thick layer of moss.

The following day was the day that Wishy Washy built her new gate.

XV

THE MEETING

The night was cold and windy. A thin layer of snow fell on the forest around the lake. It had stopped by morning. When Sue and Sam stepped out of their tepee they left footprints in the snow. They soon made many of the same discoveries about snow that children do. They made and threw snowballs. They slid down hills on leaves. They ate snow. They ran and rolled in it.

A light gust of wind brought down a shower of snow from the trees, and a large brown and yellow maple leaf, carried by the wind, fell to the ground right on top of Sue. She was flattened in the snow by the heavy, wet and cold leaf that covered her like a collapsed tent. She crawled out from under without any real damage, however, and she and Sam laughed about the incident. When they were thoroughly wet and cold, it felt good to go in and warm up by the fire.

As the day advanced, the sun warmed the air and earth and water. The thin layer of snow disappeared from the places where the sun touched. The trees began to drip.

"Sam," said Sue, "we'd better get some more firewood."

"All right," said Sam, who'd actually been thinking about a nap.

The two took axes and machetes and went to the edge of the forest. Sue and Sam needed so little wood that it was not long before they'd collected enough dry twigs. They bound the twigs together in two bundles with blackberry twine and carried them home on their heads.

Evening grew near and Sue and Sam built up their fire for heat and light. They used a fallen leaf for a door to their tepee. They closed it and sat by the fire.

Sam said, "I wonder about those letters we get from the jay. Do you think that the bird wants to help us? How does he know so much?"

"I don't know," said Sue, "maybe we will find out all about it some day."

The cold autumn night brought an end to one more day by the lake for Sue and Sam.

The following morning was cold and clear. Frost coated leaves and tree limbs, and standing water had a thin coat of ice. Smoke rose into the cloudless sky from the bird stove pipe ornament on the Wishy Washy Witch's frosty roof. Before the sun shone on the horizon, Wishy Washy was up and getting ready for her trip to find Sue and Sam. She sipped tea by her fire and thought and made plans. When it was light enough she went out to tend the animals and to get a sense of the day and the weather.

Wishy Washy came back to her cabin with a bucket of wishing well water. She put some beans on to soak in a pot for a later meal, and cooked herself some oatmeal with dried apples and ate breakfast. A few spoonsful of oatmeal remained in the pot on purpose, as this was for Sugarplum and with sugar on it, was one of his favorite foods. Wishy Washy preferred her own with honey, but the jay seemed always to make a terrible mess of it this way, and usually got it on his feathers.

Wishy Washy thought that she might have to attract Sue and Sam to her with food as if they were wild birds or animals.

She got out a small back pack and in it she put a jar of honey, some chocolate chip cookies, some extra socks for herself and a lunch for her to share with her dogs.

Earlier Wishy Washy had put a handful of donkey oats in her bird feeder outside. When among the birds that came to eat was a stellar jay, she went out and called to it in jay talk to send Sugarplum to her. Sugarplum had a very different name in jay language, a name that people can neither pronounce nor spell properly, except for Wishy Washy, who had spent years studying Stellar speech.

The jay flew off on its errand, and within the hour, Sugarplum appeared at Wishy Washy's window. She let the bird in, and gave it the oatmeal and apple cereal she had saved. Wishy Washy explained while the bird ate. "I want you to go to Sue and Sam again, this time along the lakeshore. I'll follow, but because you are so much faster than I, you'll have to stop every little way for me to catch up."

Wishy Washy put on her coat, hat and small backpack and fastened her machete around her waist for cutting her way through brush should it be necessary. She made a final check on the donkey and goats, leaving them hay, and left a note at the wishing well saying that she would be away for the day. She started off along the path to the lake with the dogs bounding ahead. Likewise, Sugarplum flew ahead, landing on branches to wait every so often while Wishy Washy caught up.

The day was cloudy, the sort of day when a light rain

shower would be no surprise, but much warmer than the previous few days. The snow had melted away.

Soon they came to the lake, which was separated from the path by a dense willow thicket. There they reached the first stream that entered the lake. By walking on a log and then taking a long jump, Wishy Washy got across the water easily. The opposite bank was thickly overgrown with thorny salmonberry bushes and devils' clubs so that she had to chop her way through for a short distance before reaching open lakeshore. And so it went, with Sugarplum flying ahead.

In places the going was hard; Wishy Washy had to climb through the tangled branches of a fallen willow tree, and take a long detour around a particularly dense thicket. In other places it was easy, she walked along the lakeshore and watched the dogs fruitlessly chase ducks. She crossed the stream represented by the middle finger on the palm of the hand map. It was shallow and wide so she waded across in her rubber boots. The stream represented by the ring finger had steep banks at the best crossing place, but after she had scrambled down she found good stepping stones for crossing the water. Using roots and vines for handholds and animal burrows for foot holds, she scrambled up the other side and sat to rest under the large maple where Sugarplum waited.

It was time for a light lunch for all of them. Wishy Washy had some of her home made dog biscuits for Marley and Bisquit. She had oats and peanut butter for Sugarplum, and some apple pie for herself. After lunch she took out a small message she had prepared and sent Sugarplum to fly ahead to give it to Sue and Sam, and then to return to her.

Sugarplum took the message and flew along the lakeshore the short distance to the next stream and then alighting on a willow branch, he watched Sue and Sam's camp. The two dolls had already brought back some fish for the day from the lake, and were now out at other activities. Soon a movement caught Sugarplum's eye; it was Sam out practicing with his bow and arrow. Then Sue came into view; she was carrying a fir cone on her head to the tepee. The jay watched until Sue reached the camp and dropped her load. He flew down from his perch, landed beside the tepee and dropped the rolled message. Sugarplum squawked once, flipped his tail up and down and flew back up to his perch.

Sue called, "Sam, the jay has come with another message. Come and see!" Sam reluctantly stopped his sport and came to the tepee. The two dolls unrolled the message.

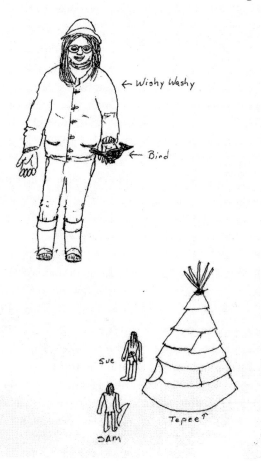

Wishy Washy had drawn a picture of herself in the clothes she was wearing that day, with Sugarplum sitting on her hand. She stood beside a tiny tepee with little figures of Sue and Sam on either side of the door.

"I don't know. . . ." began Sam as he looked at the drawing, "what this is." He was pointing at Wishy Washy, "It's like that bear that was getting honey. See how big it is next to us and the jay."

"But it's like us too," said Sue. "See how it stands up, and has a face like ours and hands. It's all covered up with something like fur or our spider web clothes."

"It's holding the jay. They must be together somehow," said Sam. "It's really big anyway," he went on, "and what does the message mean? Is this thing coming here to us?"

At this point Sugarplum gave a squawk, dived low over Sue and Sam, then rose into the air to return to Wishy Washy who was resting under a large, leafless maple tree with the dogs. A light drizzle was beginning to fall.

Sugarplum landed on a twig above Wishy Washy's head, and signaled her to come. She was ready, and giving each of her dogs a cookie, she ordered them to stay and wait for her.

Then, following Sugarplum, she walked through grass and low bushes until she saw Sugarplum land above the tepee. Wishy Washy began reciting the magic chant she had used to put life into Sue and Sam after she had made them:

"Fallen branch from a special tree,
carved with love into what you'll be.
Song of springtime, song of fall.
Growth rings circle through them all.
Painted eyes so you can see.
Gently shaped, your limbs move free.
Summer sun and winter snow.
Through your learning you will grow."

The two dolls heard the voice in the distance and were calmed and reassured by it. It was something like a memory, but not quite. Wordlessly, they came out of their shelter and looked toward the voice.

Here came the huge creature, big as a tree, toward them. The voice from above said, "Sue and Sam, I made you. I am Wishy Washy and the jay has brought you messages from me since I lost you."

The two dolls were amazed, but in fact everything in their short lives so far had been new and amazing. They were trusting and believing in Wishy Washy, for they knew nothing else. Sue shouted up at Wishy Washy, "You made us and here we are. What's next?"

Sam added, "Are you going to stay with us now?"

Wishy Washy said to the dolls, "I want to bring you home with me. It'll be warm there, with plenty to eat, and you'll learn many things."

Sue and Sam whispered back and forth and then agreed to go with Wishy Washy. She took off her backpack and then picked up the tepee and turned it upside down like a basket. She put some grass inside, then Sue and Sam's moss bedding. She picked up their tools, bow and pot of gold, and put them in too. The continuing drizzle extinguished the tiny fire.

Last of all, Wishy Washy picked up Sue and Sam, placed them in on their bedding, put the tepee in her backpack, shouldered it and headed back to where she had left the dogs. Sugarplum led again on the return trip to make sure Wishy Washy didn't lose her way.

XVI

HOME

Wishy Washy and the dogs made their way back through the rain, along the lake, and across the streams the way they had come. The witch had to close up the cover of her back pack to keep it dry inside. Sue and Sam rode in the dark.

As it was getting late and the clouds were thick, it started getting dark for Wishy Washy and the rest of her group before they reached home. There was still light when they crossed the last of the streams. After that it grew darker, the path became more well trodden and familiar. Sugarplum disappeared in the darkness, his dark blue and black feathers made him invisible.

At last they heard Dido's braying. The keen-eared animal had heard their approach in spite of the noise of the rain. He had missed Wishy Washy and the dogs, and was hungry. Soon, too, could be heard the piteous bleating of the goats.

Mostly by feel, Wishy Washy took the final steps to her door. She went inside and turned on a light. Home at last! But she must go right out again to care for the animals. What to do with Sue and Sam? There was still a faintly glowing coal among the ashes of her morning fire. Wishy Washy took off her backpack and brought out Sue and Sam, blinking in the light. They watched as she dropped some wood shavings on the coal in the fireplace and then blew on it with her bellows until the shavings burst into flame.

Wishy Washy said, "Sue and Sam, you take care of this fire, I know you know how. I have to go out again for a little while."

She left the dolls on the hearth after showing them where the firewood was kept. She got her lantern ready and went out to give oats to Dido and the two goats, who were all delighted to see her. Then she served a plate of food to each of the dogs.

She called Sugarplum, and his answering squawk came from a cross member under the roof over the well, where he was roosting for the night. She brought him a spoonful of dog food for his supper.

Then Wishy Washy was ready to go back to Sue and Sam, and to her fire so she could dry out.

She found the two dolls sitting right in the fireplace with a tiny blaze between them. They were looking around the room with puzzlement and curiosity. Wishy Washy moved them to a safe place and built up her fire large enough to heat the room. She set a pot of soup next to the fire to heat, and then went to change into dry clothes.

When the soup was warm she served herself a bowl, and she put a half a spoonful into the pot of gold for Sue and

Sam. They knew nothing of spoons, even if Wishy Washy had some small enough for them. Instead, they dipped their hands into the pot and drank out of cupped palms.

When they were finished, they were quite a mess, as it was thick pea soup. Wishy Washy gave them a bowl of warm water to wash in. Sue and Sam were so overcome with the strangeness of their new surroundings that they couldn't even ask any questions. They just looked, wide-eyed at the light, the (to them) huge fire, furniture, books and other articles in the room. Wishy Washy set up their tepee on the floor in front of the fireplace and put all their possessions inside. She told Sue and Sam to go in and go to bed, and when they seemed settled, she went off to bed herself.

The next morning Wishy Washy found the very leather pouch that Sue and Sam had been in the day that they were lost. She hung it around her neck, put Sue and Sam inside, and let them ride along with her while she fed the goats and donkey and did some other morning chores.

She took them to the wishing well and let them look in to see how far it was down to the water. She warned them against playing on the edge of the well where they might fall in.

The day was cloudy, but it was not raining and was fairly warm, so after breakfast, Wishy Washy with her dogs, took the other animals out for a walk in the woods. Sue and Sam rode along in the pouch, and when the witch sat on a log to let the animals browse on blackberry vines, Sue and Sam could get out of the pouch to play and watch the animals. Sugarplum had been following the walk through the tree tops. Wishy Washy called him to her, and giving him a piece of cookie, thanked him for his help with Sue and Sam and told him he was free to go on with his own business. He nodded his head at Sue and Sam and flew off.

After they returned home from the walk, Wishy Washy and Sue and Sam sat in front of the fire and finished the pea soup for lunch. Sue and Sam began asking questions about many things around them; about Wishy Washy's cats, about the light, about Wishy Washy's clothes, so many questions, which Wishy Washy answered as best she could. Their discussion was interrupted by the tinkling of the well bell and the barking dogs. Wishy Washy told Sue and Sam to wait by the fire.

It was Ms. Weed. She had come to make a wish, and as she lived in town, she had stopped at the post office on the way to bring Wishy Washy's mail. There was only one letter. It was from Santa. Wishy Washy thanked Ms. Weed for it, and put it in her pocket. Ms Weed wanted to gossip and make small talk, but when she asked Wishy Washy what was new with her, the witch talked of her preparations for winter and didn't mention Sue and Sam.

Ms. Weed wanted to wish for snow for Christmas, "Because it would be so pretty," she said. Wishy Washy agreed but pointed out some of the difficulties people and animals would have when the snow fell. Ms. Weed decided to make the wish anyway and finally was ready to start back home.

Wishy Washy was eager to read her letter and went back into the house by the fire to read it with Sue and Sam.

The letter was written on the back of a sheet of Christmas wrapping paper. Santa wrote:

> "Dear Wishy Washy,
>
> I plan to come and visit you in a few days to pick up my winter suit and other laundry, and to leave some more for you to do. I really appreciate this work you have done for me. You can imagine how hard it is to do laundry here at the North Pole. We don't even have the electricity to spare for a washing machine and clothes dryer; even to melt enough ice to make the water for laundry is wasteful of energy here.

When I saw you last I was complaining about the problems I was having with dolls. Well, I may have the problem solved. A family of forest elves arrived here from the south. They said that their forest had been cut down and that they had nowhere to live or any work to do. I trained them in taking charge of the dolls and they are doing fine. I guess they will stay with me until their forest grows back.

Anyway, expect me soon; I'll be there with bells on as the saying goes.

Merry Christmas

Santa"

On finishing reading the letter, Wishy Washy realized with alarm that she did not have Santa's laundry ready for him. In fact, she had dropped the sack he left with her in a corner months before, and after starting with Sue and Sam, she forgot it completely.

She said, "Come with me here in my coat pocket, Sue and Sam, we must hurry and do Santa's laundry."

She found the sack, with Santa's red winter suit right on top, and took it out back of her cabin to the washing machine.

Sue and Sam said, "Can we help?" and Wishy Washy replied, "Thank you, but this is too dangerous for you to help with today. You just watch."

She took the dolls from her pocket and put them in a bag with clothes pins that hung on the line. They could put their heads out the top to see, but could not fall in the washing machine here.

Wishy Washy put the clothes in the machine with water and soap and turned it on. As it sloshed the clothes back and forth, it sounded almost like it were saying, "Wishy Washy, Wishy Washy, Wishy Washy." She did a few steps of her washing machine dance. Then Wishy Washy said, "Sue and Sam, we'll let the machine work for a while by itself now, but we'll soon come back to finish because we must get these clothes clean and dry as soon as possible because Santa can come at any time!"

"What now?" asked Sam.

"Do we go fishing?" asked Sue.

"No," said Wishy Washy, "it's too late to go fishing, and I have plenty of food for us all. It's time to go feed the goats and the donkey again. Come into my pocket here, and we'll go care for them."

She put the dolls in her pocket and they went off to the goat house.

After the animals were tended, she set Sue and Sam on a log near the woodshed where they could watch her split firewood. They rode in her pocket while she carried wood into the house and stacked it by her hearth. Then it was time to wring out the clothes, rinse them and wring them out again. When the clothes were ready to dry, Wishy Washy brought the basket into the cabin. She hung the clothes all around the room so that they would dry even if it rained. The red suit, of heavy wool, she hung right by the fireplace and she hung Santa's red socks by the chimney with care.

"Rain!" cried Sue as a drip from the hanging clothes landed on her.

"All right," said Wishy Washy, "Sue, you and Sam go into your tepee now where the drips won't hit you. I have to make a fire and start cooking. I'll call you when it's time to bring the animals their evening oats."

And so it was. Later, after dark, while the three of them sat near Wishy Washy's fire, and the wet clothes had stopped dripping, Sue and Sam sang the song about Sue going fishing, and one about the lake with lots of duck quacks. They all laughed and had a fine time and Wishy Washy made popcorn.

XVII

SANTA'S VISIT

The next morning was foggy, with a coating of frost on the tree tops and open ground. After breakfast, Wishy Washy and Sue and Sam sat by the fire. Wishy Washy praised Sue and Sam for understanding and following the instructions that she had given them in her messages. She praised their inventiveness in making the machetes, bow and arrows and spider web clothes and generally how capable they were at surviving in the wild.

"But," she continued, "you'll need some clothes that are stronger and longer lasting than spider web to get through the winter. I'm going to make you each a suit out of this pair of gloves."

She had a pair of ladies gloves of fine kidskin. There was a hole worn in the tip of one finger of one glove. Wishy Washy had found them left behind by someone at the wishing well. Since they were too small to fit Wishy Washy's hands, why, Sue and Sam could wear them.

With a little cutting and fitting and sewing, Wishy Washy soon had a fine leather suit for each doll, and there was enough scrap left over to make a pair of simple shoes for each of them. Wishy Washy brought a mirror so that Sue and Sam could admire themselves in their new clothes.

All this time Santa's clothes had been drying by the fire and were nearly ready to take down except for the red suit which was still quite damp.

Wishy Washy continued talking to Sue and Sam, who were silently taking it all in and wriggling their toes in their new shoes. "I'll teach you to read. It's like seeing animal tracks in the sand and telling which animal it was and what it was doing. I'll teach you to write and about numbers and how to paint pictures . . ." The morning passed as Wishy Washy told the dolls stories of Santa and of the long friendship she had had with him since she was a little girl.

When this had all been told, the three of them were ready to go outside, though it was cold. Sue and Sam rode in Wishy Washy's pocket while she walked with the donkey, goats and dogs out to a good browsing spot in the woods. When they reached it, Sue and Sam could come out of the pocket and explore and play in the very spot where they were first lost.

It was not warm and the sky was starting to darken with clouds before they had been out very long. Wishy Washy did not want to be caught out in the rain, so she led the animals homeward. Sue and Sam wanted to ride Dido, so she put them on his head where they could hold on to his mane and halter. Both dolls thought that this way of travel was much more fun than riding in Wishy Washy's pocket.

When they reached home, Dido started pawing the ground, and soon lay down to roll. Wishy Washy called to the dolls to jump off his head and run to her so they wouldn't be rolled on. When the animals were settled in, Wishy Washy and the dolls went into the cabin to make up the fire and have lunch.

In the afternoon, Wishy Washy moved the dolls' te-pee out of the way, to a warm corner to one side of her fireplace. Sue and Sam remade their beds and stored their tools.

Now that Sue and Sam lived with Wishy Washy, every-thing they needed was provided. Sue told her, "We don't have anything to do. When we lived by the lake we had to keep finding food. Now with you we have everything. We don't even have to make a fire. But it feels good to have some work to do."

"I've been thinking the same thing," said Wishy Washy, "and I have an idea. You shall have your own house, and take care of yourselves."

She brought out a wooden house that was just the right size for Sue and Sam. It had been Sugarplum's house when he stayed with her and had hung in a tree outside her door. Now he lived on his own and didn't need it. Wishy Washy explained how it needed a lot of work to fix it up for a doll house. It was built of split cedar shakes. Some had come off and needed to be re-placed. It needed cleaning, a good door, windows, fur-niture, a fireplace and chimney. Sue and Sam were ex-cited by the idea.

"We can make chairs and a table like you have, only smaller," said Sam.

"We can paint pictures for the walls," said Sue.

Wishy Washy gave each doll a stiff feather so that they

could start in sweeping the floor and brushing out the corners. This kept them busy until bed time.

The next morning it was raining lightly. Wishy Washy and the dolls got up and went out to feed the animals then returned to the cabin to make their fire and have breakfast. Sue and Sam were excited over their ideas for fixing up their house.

They were all talking about it when they heard a lot of noise outside. Barking, braying and bleating accompanied by jingling bells made Wishy Washy think that someone had come to wish at the well. She grabbed her hat and coat and went out to calm the animals and found that it was Santa who had arrived. He set his sleigh down right beyond the wishing well.

Santa greeted Wishy Washy and gave her a hug. His beard was wet from the rain. Santa was wearing his ordinary winter clothes, for he wore his red suit, which Wishy Washy had washed, only on Christmas.

"Why don't you unhitch those deer?" said Wishy Washy. So Santa did. The eight reindeer would visit, play and eat hay with Dido, Ahmed and Patina while Santa and Wishy Washy visited. The two of them walked to the cabin accompanied by the joyful dogs.

In the cabin, Sue and Sam waited in anticipation to meet Santa, who was to be, in fact, only the second person they had ever met. When Santa came in and Wishy Washy had offered him a seat, she said, "Santa, I want you to meet Sue and Sam," and placed them on a table near his chair.

Sam stepped forward and said, "Hello Santa, I'm Sam," and Sue likewise said, "Santa, I'm Sue."

Santa said, "Well, I have a lot of dolls, but no two like you."

Wishy Washy told Santa something of the story of Sue and Sam and how they had been made for him, but that now

Wishy Washy was glad that they had a chance to stay with her for as long as they liked.

As she talked, Wishy Washy was gathering Santa's laundry from the places she had hung it to dry. She was folding it and packing it in Santa's sack. Last of all came the red suit, which was dry now. She folded it and placed it at the top of the sack.

"Thank you for the laundry, Wishy Washy," said Santa, "what do you want for Christmas?"

"Having Sue and Sam here with me is enough of a gift for me," said Wishy Washy, "but I'll whisper some things in your ear that would be nice for them to have," and so she did, and Santa smiled and nodded.

Next, Wishy Washy served them all some cookies and tea. Sue and Sam ate only a few cookie crumbs. They brought their hazel nut shells from the tepee to drink tea from.

Soon it was time for Santa to leave. The rain had stopped but it was getting to be late in the afternoon.

Outside Santa lit his pipe and called the reindeer by name to take their places in front of the sleigh. Dido was glad to see them go, because he did not feel generous about sharing his hay.

Santa took a sack of dirty laundry from the sleigh to give to Wishy Washy, saying that he'd be by one of these days after Christmas for it. He placed his sack of clean laundry with the precious red suit in the sleigh, while Ahmed skillfully picked his pocket of a candy cane.

When Santa went to hitch up his team, he found there was an extra member. Patina stood in line with the reindeer, eager for a new adventure.

Santa said, "I'm sorry, Patina, but you can't fly. You have to stay here, but I know you've been good (giving a wink) and I'll bring you something nice for Christmas, and for you too, Ahmed, and Dido, Bisquit and Marley. I'll bring a merry Christmas to you all, in just a few more days." With that, he sprang into the sleigh and whistled to the reindeer. Magically they rose into the sky and quickly disappeared through the low cloud.

Wishy Washy was left holding Sue and Sam in her hands. She put them in her pocket and picked up the sack of laundry. As she walked toward the washing machine, she said, half to herself and half to Sue, Sam and the dogs, "Let me think, what can I make for a Christmas present for Santa?"

The End . . .

for now . . .

Wishy Washy's Chant

Music by Dianne Everson

About the Collaborative Creators of Wishy Washy's Wish

Walter Barkas and Rivkah Sweedler are two artists who lived in the forests of the Pacific Northwest in cabins they built of fir poles, logs and cedar shakes.

They began their collaboration of life and art in 1978. Their stories, sculptures, paintings, photographs, living spaces, all evolved as egalitarian collaborations.

They shared a basic desire to learn, experiment, have fun and do their best. The goal was to live by their own skills as much as possible using the windfalls of nature and the cast off windfalls of the consumer society. To live IN the forest and harvest FROM the forest without destroying or "civilizing" the forest.

Walter died in 1995. The collaboration continues as Rivkah puts together and completes the stories and adventures.

What if
wishy washy
didn't send
letters to
Sue and
Sam?

CPSIA information can be obtained
at www.ICGtesting.com
Printed in the USA
FFOW02n2224260618
47249634-50119FF